RECKLESS

Sydney Campbell

ISBN: 978-1-990231-00-1

Cover design by abu-chan
Editing by Megan Records

This is a work of fiction. Unless otherwise indicated, all the names, characters, businesses, places, events and incidents in this book are either the product of the author's imagination or used in a fictitious manner. Any resemblance to actual persons, living or dead, or actual events is purely coincidental.

For my mother, who would've laughed at
the whole endeavor.

Other books by Sydney Campbell:

Allie Styles Romance Series:
Temptation (Book 1)
Deception (Book 2)
Reckonings (Book 3)
Beginnings (Book 4)

Courtyard Tales of Contemporary Romance
Reawakening
Redemption
Reckless

CHAPTER ONE

Hailey

I stood in front of my hallway mirror, making one final assessment before heading out. My hair was in place, my make-up perfect, and I looked fabulous. I wiped the lipstick from the corner of my mouth with my thumb, grabbed my favourite over-sized bag, and walked out the door.

It was the first Sunday in January and it was damn cold. Thankfully, I didn't have far to go. I was heading over to meet my new neighbours, Allie and Matt. When you lived in a courtyard with ten houses, it was difficult to avoid getting to know everyone. Jason and Rob, the couple who lived in the house attached to Allie and Matt's, had told me they were a lot of fun. They'd moved in a couple of months ago, and apparently had just come back from their honeymoon the previous night. I hadn't yet met them, but I'd seen them in the courtyard. They were an adorable couple, and it was nice to have some fresh blood around.

Not that the other neighbours weren't great. Rob and Jason were amazing. And the Tates, well, they were the Tates. Zach Abrams, the music producer, pretty much kept to himself, and Casey, the house-sitter next door, was just a kid. And that Catholic couple was a little too weird for me. I had zero patience for the Marshalls and their kids, and I couldn't even remember the last time I'd seen Louisa, the woman who lived in the corner house.

I made a mental note to bring a doggy bag to the Levinsons, the 86- and 88-year-old brother and sister who lived next door. I knew they wouldn't be going, and I also knew how lucky I was to have them as neighbours. So quiet I never heard a thing. Unless it was their smoke alarm, which went off constantly. The last time it happened, Mr. Levinson's daughter confided to me that one more time and she was moving them in with her. As much as I knew it was for the best, I still dreaded it. Who knew who'd buy the house? For that reason, I made sure to check on them daily, bringing food and puzzles to keep them busy.

I walked up the steps and was about to ring the bell when the door swung open. Allie stood there with a smile, a glass in her hand. She was adorable. Brown, naturally curly hair, dark eyes, a killer body. I instantly craned my neck for a better look at Matt, but he was nowhere to be seen.

"Hailey, right? So glad you could come! This is such a nice surprise."

Allie reached out her hand and I laughed, hugging her instead. She stiffened in surprise, then embraced me with both arms. I never did anything half-assed.

"Congratulations! I hear you got married. Or should I say mazel tov?" I asked.

"Either is appropriate. Matt's Jewish, I'm not. Come on in."

Allie moved aside to let me in. I was one of the last to arrive, and the margaritas and food were flowing. I turned to smile at her.

"Matt's mixing drinks in the kitchen. Go on. I know you know the way."

Allie laughed and then turned as the doorbell rang.

I wandered into the kitchen, through all the boxes and *stuff* taking up most of the room. Matt was at the counter, pouring margaritas from a pitcher. He looked up when I walked in and *dang*, he was hot. Not Zach hot, but definitely fantasy material. He and Allie seemed to be around my age; maybe Matt was a little older. I'd have to ask Rob at some point.

"You must be Hailey! Welcome! Want a drink?"

"I would love one, Matt. Thank you. Pleasure to meet you."

I walked over and since he was pouring, I just leaned over and planted a kiss on his cheek. He turned red. *Adorable.* He passed me the drink and got busy talking to Jason, who gave me a look that said *Don't even bother.* Like I'd ever try to break up a couple. Cheating was not my thing.

I spotted Sophia Tate across the room and she nodded. I smiled back but made no move toward her. She got the message. The Tates had an open marriage and zero shame about inviting people in. I was not interested.

Just then, I heard Zach's voice behind me and turned towards him. I walked over and slid my hand over his shoulder, purring into his ear.

"Zach. How are you?"

He politely ducked out from under my hand and flashed that dazzling smile at me. The man was a god; tall, built, tattooed with the sexiest damn ring on his thumb. But he was also damaged goods, and therefore off my naughty list. He wouldn't even look twice at me, and I knew better than to get involved. I had a strict in-and-out policy and I made sure both parties understood the rules. Zach was not a one-night stand. So instead, I just enjoyed making him nervous.

"Hi, Hailey. You're looking great tonight."

I tilted my head and eyed him. Just then Casey came up to join us and started talking Zach's ear off. I rolled my eyes, not particularly caring if she noticed. She was a kid, late twenties, and completely lost. By the time I was her age, I was well-established in my field, and now, at 32, I owned my own marketing firm. She was just a house-sitter.

I grabbed a seat on the couch and listened to the guys talk sports for a while, kind of zoning out. I hadn't gotten much sleep the night before. I was dealing with a difficult client on an impossible deadline. I knew I'd only stay a few more minutes before bringing a plate over to the Levinsons and heading home. I sat back, sipped my drink, and enjoyed the show.

*

Hours later, I was curled up on the couch watching reruns of *Schitt's Creek* with a tub of chocolate therapy ice cream. As far as I was concerned, David and Patrick had the best TV relationship of all-time, and I could get lost in that show for hours. I wasn't a romantic, but something about the way they came together and completed each other always moved me. And I wasn't easily moved.

When I'd had my fill, I tossed the pint container and climbed the stairs to bed. It had been a long day, and I had a huge Monday coming up with my client. I needed a good night's rest. As soon as I finished up in the bathroom, I crawled into bed and pulled up the covers. But sleep wouldn't come.

Putting total faith in my trusty battery-operated friend, I reached over to my night-table drawer. This was nothing a good orgasm wouldn't fix. I was just stressed out and needed a release. Knowing I usually passed out right after, I grabbed my earplugs and put them in so nothing would wake me until morning.

I was so wound up it only took me a few minutes to get off, and while not completely satisfied, it was enough to do the trick. I rolled over, closed my eyes, and fell asleep.

CHAPTER TWO

Sam

It was the last call of my last shift of the week. A small kitchen fire had set off the smoke detector at 1:00 a.m., waking an elderly couple and scaring them half to death. Christ, the last thing I needed on a Sunday night was to have two seniors die on me. We had just gotten things under control and we were heading back to the truck. I was picking up my ax when the woman, a Mrs. Levinson, stopped me. She reached out and put her hand on my arm, giving me a concerned look.

"What about Hailey?" she asked.

"I'm sorry, ma'am, who's Hailey?" I asked, trying to be patient.

There were only two people in the house. I knew this. Maybe she was having hallucinations. Or had some form of dementia. I didn't know. I just wanted to get back to the fire station, get out of my gear, and go home. It had been a long week. I'd just been given notice to vacate the house I was renting—the owners' daughter was moving in. I needed to find a place to live and fast. I had no time for imaginary people.

"Hailey, next door. She never came out of the house. What if something caught in the walls?"

I sighed and looked at her; she was clearly worried.

"Ma'am, everyone came out. We knocked on all the doors. She must be out."

The old woman shook her head furiously.

"No, Hailey came by and brought us dinner, then went home. And sometimes she sleeps with earplugs. She always checks on us when the smoke detector goes off. *Always*. Please go check."

I smiled thinly and walked over to the truck. The guys were all climbing on.

"Hey, I'm going to check on the neighbour. Give me a minute, okay?"

Chuck nodded at me and I turned back towards the courtyard. I got to the door in question and knocked. Nothing. I rang. Nothing. I looked over at the old lady, who was nodding at me, encouraging me to go in. She handed me a key. I cursed silently and slipped the key in the lock.

The inside of the house was dark, save for a light coming from the kitchen. I walked over and peered in. Empty. The rest of the floor was open-concept, and I could see there was no one there. I walked briskly up the stairs, very fucking anxious to get gone. I flipped on the hallway light. I stuck my head into the bathroom and each of the first two bedrooms. Nothing. There was some smoke in the house, but there was no real danger. Nobody would've slept through the commotion, though.

I stuck my head into the last door, and to my fucking disbelief, saw a shape under the covers in the light coming from the hallway. *Fucking hell.*

"Hey," I called, then again, a little louder. "Hey!"

Nothing. *Crap.* Fed up at this point, I flipped on the light and yelled.

"HEY! GET UP!"

The woman shot up straight out of bed, covers dropping to her waist, terror in her eyes and screaming like a banshee. She moved her head around blindly, searching for something. Finding it, she fucking launched it at me. It hit me right in the head and landed at my feet. She was still screaming at me to get out as I bent down to retrieve the object.

I held it in my hand, studying it until I realized what it was. A fucking vibrator. The woman threw a sex toy at me. *Well, this is new.* I ignored her screaming, scratched my head, and turned it on. I had to smile.

"OH MY GOD, what are you doing?" she cried.

I looked at her and held up the toy.

"This any good?" I asked casually.

She threw the covers back and got out of bed. I took a step back. She was fucking hot. Tall, dark hair, and smoldering eyes. Sex on a stick. She was wearing nothing but a big white V-neck T-shirt and white panties. Christ. I swallowed.

"Who the fuck are you and what are you doing in my bedroom?"

She was advancing fast, but I held my ground. I was still a good five or six inches taller than her. I pointed to my uniform.

"Fireman. I came in here to save your ass, but apparently, you're just fine."

Her anger turned to shock, then concern.

"The Levinsons! Are they okay?"

She looked around frantically and grabbed a sweatshirt and sweatpants. She was pulling them on, muttering to herself. She went from hard as nails to soft as a kitten in two seconds flat. I reached out and touched her arm.

"Hey, they're fine. It's all over. You slept through the whole thing."

She pulled her arm away, letting out a long breath. She took a moment to calm down, then looked me up and down appraisingly.

"Fireman, huh?" A slow grin spread across her face.

Now, that's the reaction I'm used to. I ran my hand over my face. Yes, she was hot but I was still on shift and beyond exhausted. Besides, I could already tell this one was trouble.

"You okay?" I asked her.

"Yeah. Am I safe?"

"From the fire? The fire is out."

She walked up to me, stopping about a foot away. She looked up at me from under her lashes and despite my best intentions to remain unaffected, there was a definite twitching in my pants.

"What about from you?" she purred.

I smiled and took a step back, aware of the rising heat between us.

"You, Trouble, are safe from me."

I handed her her vibrator, which she took without comment. Walking out the door, I paused in the hallway and turned back.

"Maybe don't sleep with the earplugs. No comment on the vibe, though. That's totally your call."

*

The old lady was still waiting for me on her front porch. She had an expectant look in her eyes, and there was another woman with her now, mid-sixties, who reached out her hand.

"Hi, I'm Sonia, Mrs. Levinson's niece. Thank you so much for coming to the rescue," she said.

"Is she okay? Is Hailey okay?"

I looked at the tiny little woman, so worried about her neighbour. If only she knew how I'd found her. I couldn't help but laugh out loud at the thought.

"She's just fine. Don't you worry. But do be safe."

"Oh, don't worry," Sonia said. "I'm getting them out of here as soon as possible. Just have to get them moved in with me and put the house on the market."

I was halfway down the walk but turned around when I heard that.

"You're going to sell this house?" I asked.

She nodded.

"I told them—one more accident and they

were moving in with me. I'm sick of worrying about them."

I studied her, then reached into my pocket and pulled out my card, walking back and handing it to her.

"Call me. We'll talk. I'm looking."

Sonia smiled widely.

"It needs a lot of work," she said.

"It's what I do. Seriously, let's talk."

"Sure thing. Anything to help out the guy who saved my dad."

I headed back to the truck, feeling a little lighter for the first time all day.

CHAPTER THREE

Hailey

Whoa.

What the hell had just happened? One minute I was fast asleep, the next, a smoking hot fireman was standing in my room. I mean, yeah, the poor Levinsons, but *fuck*. A flesh-and-blood fireman. He was about half a foot taller than me and built like a house. I couldn't see anything through his gear, but my mind was full of ideas of what he looked like naked. Sandy brown hair, light-coloured eyes. Rawr. He was hot.

And I threw my vibrator at him.

Christ.

One day I'd laugh about it, but today wasn't that the day. There was no way I was getting back to sleep. My heart was pounding. That was hands-down the scariest thing that had ever happened to me. Followed by potentially the hottest. But whatever.

I went downstairs into the kitchen to put on the kettle for some cocoa. While waiting for the water to boil, I rolled a joint and put on my coat and boots. Cocoa made, joint ready, I went out onto the back deck and brushed the snow off the chair I kept out there for exactly these purposes.

My deck looked out over the back alley that ran behind the courtyard in a U-shape. Across the alley were trees that hid a parking lot belonging to the ice rink on the other side. While the winter traffic was a pain in the ass, it gave us residents a lot of privacy we wouldn't otherwise find in the trendy neighbourhood of NDG. I smoked the joint slowly, silently going over my presentation for the morning.

The hairs on the back of my neck stood when I heard the sound of gravel crunching down the alley toward the sidewalk. Someone, or something, was coming. I reached behind me, putting my hand on the doorknob in case I needed a quick escape. I was relatively safe on my deck, but it was low enough that a determined stranger could scramble up.

I heard a male voice quietly cursing, and then a flashlight switching on. I jumped up.

"Who's there?" I called.

All I heard was a chuckle.

"Trouble? That you?"

Out of the darkness came the fireman. He was dressed in jeans and a black leather jacket, a beanie sitting snug on his head.

"What the hell are you doing here?" I asked.

He stopped for a moment. I couldn't see his face, as he was shining his flashlight towards me. I shielded my eyes with my hand and after a moment, he dropped the beam to the ground.

"One of my buddies dropped his flashlight. Told him I'd come look for it on the way home."

He looked around a bit.

"Doesn't seem to be here," he concluded.

He glanced at me.

"You smoking weed?"

I took stock of him, wrapping my coat tighter around me.

"Yeah. You want some?"

He checked the alley, came closer to the railing of my deck, and eyed it. He took a step back and then, putting his hands on the ledge, hopped up over the side. *Holy fuck*. That was a panty-dropping move.

I stood up and held out the joint as he wiped the snow off his jeans. He shook his head.

"Nah, thanks. But I'll keep you company."

His fingers brushed lightly against mine as he pushed my hand away. I was glad for the darkness so he couldn't see me blush. I *never* blushed.

I took a lazy drag on the joint, eyeing him the entire time. He shifted his gaze, watching the smoke drift off into the cold night air.

"What are you doing up?" he asked.

"Couldn't sleep," I said.

"Yeah. Adrenaline gets going after something like that."

He stepped closer to me, taking the joint from my lips and tossing it off the deck.

"Gets your heart racing, blood pumping," he whispered.

My jaw tightened as I fought to hide any reaction. My heart *was* racing, but I sure as hell wasn't going to tell him that. He reached over and adjusted the collar of my coat, letting his fingers skim down my jaw as he moved away. Despite the frigid temperature, there was definite heat between us. I shifted uncomfortably, trying to squeeze my thighs together without him noticing.

I stepped back and indicated the chair.

"Have a seat. I'll go in and get another chair."

He grinned and sat down. As I moved past him to go inside, he snaked his arm around my waist and pulled me onto his lap. My breath caught and my nipples instantly hardened against the thin cotton of the T-shirt I wore under my jacket.

"Is your heart racing, Trouble?"

I looked him in the eye, saying nothing. He reached up and placed his fingers on my neck, feeling my pulse.

"Yeah, your heart's racing, all right."

He placed his hand on the side of my head, pulling me closer towards him. I closed my eyes and felt his mouth on mine. He ran his tongue along my lower lip, and I wrapped my arms around his neck, swinging one leg over his lap so I was straddling him. He put his other arm around my waist, drawing me in close.

I parted my lips slightly, and he deepened the kiss, sliding his tongue into my mouth and making my head swim. I moaned and he pulled me in even closer. I could feel him getting hard against me and I pressed up against him, grinding into him until a low growl started deep in his chest.

"You don't even know my name," I breathed.

"Hailey. But I can already tell you'll always be Trouble to me."

He wrapped his hand around the back of my

head, his lips meeting mine again. I had no choice but to kiss him back. I pulled his hat off, running my fingers through his hair. He groaned, driving his tongue deeper, taking everything I had to offer him.

"Inside," he commanded.

I slid off his lap, turning to open the door. It never even occurred to me to say no. This was most definitely going to happen. A fireman! This was like a Top 5 fantasy. I couldn't fucking wait to slide down his pole.

I opened the door and motioned for him to go into the kitchen. I followed him and closed the door behind us, making sure to lock it. I planned on leading him into the living room, towards softer and warmer terrain. But when I turned around, he was right there, and he grabbed my hips, pinning me up against the patio doors.

I just had time to catch my breath before he moved in to kiss me again. Damn, he knew how to kiss. Just the feel of his lips on mine was enough to push every one of my buttons. I was practically squirming and I could feel how wet I was already.

He unzipped my coat and slid it off my shoulders, all without breaking the kiss. When it fell to the floor, he stepped back for a moment to look at me in my thread-bare T-shirt and sweats. There was hunger in his eyes. It was such a turn-on I reached out for him, pulling him closer. He kissed my neck, running his tongue along the soft skin near my shoulder. I shivered as he slid his hand under my shirt and cupped my breast.

"Trouble, you've got some nice tits," he whispered in my ear.

I moaned in response. He lifted my shirt and ducked his head, taking my nipple in his mouth, his gentle licking rapidly turning into an insistent biting. I lifted one leg, wrapping it around his waist, driving myself into him. He pushed it back down, planting it firmly on the ground as he dropped to his knees. I sighed as he pulled down my sweats, followed by my panties.

"*Fuck*," he moaned. "I can *see* how wet you are."

He grabbed my ass with both hands as he buried his head between my legs. He took one slow, long lick from bottom to top and I threw my head back against the glass as his tongue landed on my clit.

"Goddammit, Fireman, that's good."

He chuckled against my skin, sending me further towards the edge. He rubbed the stubble of his jaw along the tender flesh of my inner thighs as he devoured me, the juxtaposition of soft and rough driving me insane.

"Slow down, slow down," I moaned. "Let's try to drag this out a little."

"Fuck no," he mumbled, doubling his efforts.

It was too late anyway. I was sailing over the cliff by this point, my entire body tensing then releasing in waves with the force of the orgasm that tore through me. He still held me firmly, sliding his tongue inside, stroking me slowly as I came down.

"Oh, god," I moaned.

"Sam. My name is Sam."

I laughed. He stood up, pulling me towards him as he reached his full height, and kissed me. I had no fucking idea what I'd just been laughing about. Once again he reached for my ass, and I stepped out of my pants before jumping up and wrapping both legs around his waist. He carried me easily over to the counter and sat me down. I reached for the hem of my shirt and pulled it over my head.

He gazed at me as he unzipped his jacket and slid it off. He then pulled off his T-shirt, exposing the most magnificent upper body I'd ever seen up close. *Holy shit*. The man's abs were so ridiculously cut I wanted to lick them. He reached for his belt and I put my hands on his to stop him. He looked at me and grinned.

I worked the buckle quickly, pulling the leather through and getting busy with the button and fly on his jeans. Within seconds I was pushing them, along with his boxer briefs, down over his hips. He stepped back and completed the job. I sucked in a sharp breath as I looked him over.

"Christ. You're beautiful."

"I'm supposed to say that to you."

"But you didn't."

"I told you you had great tits."

I rolled my eyes.

"What's the matter, did I threaten your masculinity by calling you beautiful?"

"Jesus, I knew you were trouble."

"You going to fuck me or are we just going to argue about this all night?"

"You're also bossy," he said.

He reached down for his jeans and pulled out his wallet. He flipped through it until he found a condom then tossed the wallet onto the counter.

"Maybe we should've exchanged a few words before jumping into this," he muttered. "I'm not sure how much I actually like you."

"Yeah, ditto, now shut up and put on the condom."

He slipped it on with a speed that only comes with much practice. He was still ready to go after my supposed affront on his manhood. He looked up at me, a little hesitant.

"Oh, come on," I said, reaching out and grabbing him by the waist and pulling him toward me.

He reached out instinctively for my breast and as he ran his thumb over my nipple, I reached down and guided him in, sliding toward the edge of the counter to take him to the hilt. His eyes flew open, and he dropped his hands, grabbing me by the waist as he began to thrust.

"You play dirty," he growled.

"I get what I want," I spat back.

He brought one hand up to the back of my head, pulling me in until his lips met mine. Unlike the tentative passion of our earlier kiss, this one was fueled by pure fire, our tongues battling for dominance. I braced my hands on the counter behind me, raising my ass so I could meet his thrusts, grinding my hips into him. I squeezed my thighs together, determined to make him lose it as quickly as I had.

"Oh, fuck," he grunted, squeezing my hips as he drove himself into me one last time. I pulled him in closer with my legs, holding him close as he rode out his orgasm. When he was done, I lowered myself back down onto the counter and dropped my legs. I gave him a push on the chest, indicating he should back off.

He snorted and moved back as I jumped down off the counter.

"Thanks, Sam. That was some pretty decent sex."

He snorted again, louder this time.

"Pretty decent? Gee, thanks, Hails."

I closed my eyes, his use of my nickname grating on me like nails on a blackboard. I bent down to pick up his clothes, fully aware of the show I was giving him. I could hear his breathing alter and grinned to myself. I stood and tossed him his clothes.

"I've got a really early morning. You leaving the way you came, or shall I show you to the front door?"

CHAPTER FOUR

Sam

There was no missing flashlight. I had no idea why I'd lied to Hailey. I'd come to check out the exterior of the Levinson house, see what kind of shape it was in before putting in an offer. I had never expected to bump into anyone, much less her.

Christ, that woman *was* trouble. Two days later and I was still thinking about fucking her on her kitchen counter. That body was smoking hot, and I was frankly surprised by how much her bossiness had turned me on. I was always the one who took charge.

I checked the time on my phone. It was close to nine a.m., and though I was sure she must've left for work already, I still wanted to wait before heading up the courtyard walk for my meeting with Sonia. I did not want to risk bumping into her. The last thing I needed was for her to think I was after her. I was actually having second thoughts about putting an offer in on the house, considering these new circumstances. But fuck it, after talking with Sonia the previous day, I knew it was a better deal than I was going to find anywhere else. For some reason, these old siblings wanted to cut me a break, given I'd been the one on call for the fire.

Considering Mr. Levinson had bought the house in 1940, whatever we settled on was guaranteed to earn him a massive profit. Hailey would just have to figure out how to deal with having me next door.

Fucking Hailey. She'd kicked me out. Like, she didn't even try to be discreet about it. This was a first for me. If anyone was eyeing the exit, it was usually me. I was going to have to rethink that, though. Being shown the door had not been a pleasant feeling.

I zipped up my jacket and got out of the car, heading for the Levinsons. Thankfully there was no one else in the courtyard. It was colder than a witch's tit, so that wasn't surprising. I raced up the steps and didn't even get a chance to knock before Sonia threw the door open with a smile.

An hour later, I walked out with the promise of a new house. My own house. My first. I still couldn't believe what happened.

Between the lack of an agent, the amount of work required on the house, the speed with which they wanted to sell, and the small factor of me having saved their lives, they sold it to me for a pittance. I had a serious talk with Sonia, not wanting to take advantage of such elderly people, but she was adamant. It was crazy. The market was at its peak. But there was no way I was walking away. I'd worry about the Hailey problem later.

I spent the rest of the week dealing with the bank and getting everything in order so we could sign the papers on Friday. Sonia was intent on getting the Levinsons moved into her house ASAP, and I was more than happy to oblige. I arranged to have my shit moved in while I was on shift the following week, and then I'd have a full week off to start renovations. It would be a pain in the ass living in the dust and plaster, but with my lease expiring at the end of January, I had no other option.

My own fucking house.

*

By the time I walked into the station on Monday morning, I was officially a homeowner. I broke the news to the guys and they were stunned. No one had seen this coming. I had famously been a drifter for a long time, only ending up in Montreal a few years ago after having been gone for over a decade. I had zero interest in committing to anything other than fighting fires.

There was still an hour or so before the shift, and Greg suggested we head to the grocery store and stock up on supplies for a celebratory dinner. We all climbed into his truck, the guys grilling me about the house. When I fessed up and told them it was the fire call from the week before, Chuck looked at me and grinned.

"What about the hot neighbour?" he asked.

I'd told him about what happened when I'd burst into Hailey's room that night, but I'd neglected to fill them in on my return visit. Screw them. Most of the guys were married and I was tired of them living vicariously through me.

"Yeah, we talked a bit afterward. Not for me. A little too bitchy, way too bossy."

Greg snorted.

"Doesn't matter how hot a girl is; somewhere, some guy is sick of her shit."

I looked at him in the seat beside me.

"You're such a pig."

He just shrugged.

Chuck pulled into the parking lot and we walked into the grocery store, Greg grabbing the cart as we headed towards the meat fridges. As we turned down the first aisle, there she fucking was.

"Oh, look," I said. "Here comes Trouble."

The guys followed my gaze, eyes landing on Hailey.

"Whoa," Greg muttered.

"She's poison, dude."

Greg looked at me.

"What happened?"

"Nothing. Shut up."

I looked away from him and towards Hailey as she stopped in front of me. She looked fantastic. Tight jeans, long fitted coat open at the neck. Boots up to her knees and all I could think about was fucking her in them, having them wrapped around my waist with those heels digging into my ass.

"Well hello, Fireman." She slowly took in Greg and Chuck, both of whom I suddenly hated with a passion. "Or should I say, Firemen?"

"Guys, this is Hailey. Hailey, Chuck and Greg."

"Hailey?" Chuck said. "You mean the neighbour?"

A sly grin spread across her face at the realization I'd told them about her. She raised her eyebrow at me and even though I wanted to look away, I held her stare.

"Does she—" Greg started and I elbowed him hard in the gut. He almost doubled over. I didn't care. This was *not* the way Hailey was finding out.

But she didn't miss a thing. She turned her attention to Greg, flashing a thousand-watt smile.

"Do I what, Fireman?"

Greg just shook his head, sputtering. I took the cart from him and started past Hailey. The guys quickly followed.

"Later, Trouble."

CHAPTER FIVE

Hailey

I left the office early on Friday and got into my car feeling lighter than I had in months. January, along with my most difficult contract to date, was officially done and in the books. Plus, I had had the foresight to book off the first two weeks of February as vacation, which I fully intended to spend in bed with ice cream and Netflix.

I pulled onto my street and was instantly annoyed to see a large moving truck parked in the only remaining permitted spots. Gritting my teeth, I circled the block again looking for parking. When I found it, I sat in the car and counted to ten, trying to collect myself before getting out. I was about to meet my new neighbour and I didn't want to get off on the wrong foot.

I pulled down the visor and checked myself in the mirror. I was still so upset about losing the Levinsons. What if the new owners had young kids? Christ. I'd had it so good. With a sense of dread, but trying to keep my steps light, I walked up to the house. Just as I got there, two of the movers came out the front door. I smiled and waved. One raised his eyebrow at me while the other said hello.

"Either of you know where the new owner is?" I asked.

Polite guy just shrugged.

"From what I know, he's not moving in until Sunday night. He gave us his key and asked us to move all the stuff in."

I stopped dead at the word "he." I tried to peek around his large frame through the open door to see if there were toys or shit.

"Single?" I asked with zero shame.

"I think so. Dude doesn't look like he lives with a broad."

I clenched my fists to keep from rolling my eyes. He was giving me information, after all.

"Okay, thanks a lot."

I turned and walked back down the steps and turned onto my own walkway. I went inside, shed my coat, and poured myself a drink.

Vacation.

*

Monday morning, my eyes shot open at the sound of some loud-as-fuck power tool working in full force next door. I rolled over and picked up my phone. 8:01 a.m. Fucking hell. This was not good.

I got out of bed and pulled on my sweats. I tied my hair up in a messy bun and raced down the stairs. I reached for my jacket as I slid on my boots. Despite how determined I'd been to get off on a good foot with my new neighbour, he'd already messed up big time.

I walked out my front door, down the steps, and then up his steps. I rang the bell then pounded on the door. I was furious. The three-second walk over had given me enough time to work myself into a nice rage. The door swung open and I was about to start yelling when my breath caught in my throat.

"FIREMAN."

He just grinned.

"Hey, Trouble."

I closed my eyes.

"Tell me you're helping a friend out by doing work on his place."

He laughed.

"Nope. Guess again."

"Fucking hell. You know it's eight o'clock in the morning, right?"

"Yeah, thing is, I only have a week off. I gotta get shit done here. And to be honest, I thought you'd have left for work by now."

I glared at him.

"I'm on a much-needed vacation."

He nodded slowly, realization sinking in.

"Ah. I see."

He shrugged.

"Sorry, Hails, I've really got to get this done. I'll try not to work on an adjoining wall, but that's the best I can do. Law is on my side here."

"Of all the fucking things that could've happened to me. I can't believe this. Let me guess, Mr. Levinson was so grateful to you he gave you the damn house."

"Almost."

"FUCK."

I turned on my heel and stormed down the steps. I could feel his eyes on me as I turned into my own house but refused to look back at him. Instead, I slammed the door behind me.

I kicked off my boots and shed my jacket, continuing into the kitchen where I filled and plugged in the kettle. All the while listening to the power drill going next door. This was going to be a long week. My only saving grace was the knowledge it would be quiet the next week, and I'd have a chance to catch up on my sleep before returning to work.

And that's when it hit me. The fireman had moved in next door. The fireman I'd fucked on this very kitchen counter. I suddenly felt very uneasy. When I was done with a guy, I liked to cut them loose. Completely. Living next door wasn't loose. It was very, very captive.

I sat down at the table and slowly sipped my tea. How the hell was I going to deal with this? It's not like I could ignore him. There was too much of a community in the courtyard to swing that. I also knew there was no way I was getting back to sleep. I wandered into the living room and settled onto the couch, flipping on the TV and turning the volume on loud. I went back to my *Schitt's Creek* reruns and pulled the blanket up over me.

*

By six o'clock, I was in a blind rage. The noise was incessant and the thought of another week of it was driving me insane. My hair was still damp from my shower, but I pulled on a pair of jeans and a sweater before going downstairs to have things out with Sam.

Once again, I pulled on my coat and boots and headed outside. He'd been at it for ten hours straight, stopping once around noon for twenty minutes. As I walked out the front door, I saw Jason and Matt chatting on the walkway, both of them returning from work.

"Hey!" Jason called. "Hails! Have you met your new—"

I stormed past him and up the steps.

"Oh, shit," Jason muttered. I heard him race up the steps behind me. He grabbed my arm before I could pound on the door.

I turned on him.

"Jason. I'm a big girl. I know what I'm doing."

"Hails. He just moved in. Give him a break. Did you even see him? *Hot!*"

"Yeah. He's a fireman."

"I KNOW!"

I almost laughed at how excited he was.

"He's an asshole, Jason. Trust me. He deserves what he's got coming."

Jason shrugged and trotted back down the stairs. Matt just stood there, watching the whole exchange with a grin on his face. Jason returned to him and they resumed their conversation, Matt keeping an eye on me as I pounded on the door. Once again, it swung open and there he was, now completely covered in plaster dust yet still managing to look off-the-charts sexy. I took a breath and shoved him inside so I could get through the door.

I walked past him into the living room then through the dining room, where he'd been at work. There was a ladder set up in the middle of the room and drop cloths over all the furniture, which was set away from the walls so he could plaster. It was a mess. I turned to him, hands on my hips.

"Listen, Fireman. You can't do this all day, every day. I'm going to go fucking crazy. It's bad enough you're living here; you don't have to make my life extra miserable."

He shrunk back, stung.

"What do you mean, 'bad enough I'm living here?'"

I sighed.

"I just meant I don't shit where I eat. If I'd have known you were buying this house, I never would've slept with you—"

"You didn't."

I stared at him.

"Semantics. Fine. I never would've fucked you. Happy? This is a rule I never break."

"Never?"

"Never."

"Even when it was oh-so-good?" he teased.

"You think I forget what you felt like under my hands? My tongue?"

I looked him up and down, though I barely needed to, having memorized every inch of his beautiful body already. I suddenly realized how close he was, and how incredibly turned on I was. Why were we talking about sex? I clenched my thighs and changed the subject.

"So what's your plan? When are you stopping for the night?"

"Right now," he growled.

He reached out and grabbed me by the hips, pulling me towards him. He crushed his lips against mine and kissed me like a man possessed. I hesitated only a millisecond before parting my lips to let him in. I pressed myself up against him, rubbing my breasts against his chest. He drew back.

"If you don't want this, tell me now," he said.

"Christ, you talk too much. Just kiss me."

I got up on my tiptoes and kissed him, wrapping my arms around his neck as he held me around the waist. He walked me backwards, not breaking the kiss, until I bumped up against something. I turned my head to see the ladder. I turned back to him and he was grinning wickedly. He pulled off my jacket and slid my jeans and panties down my legs, all before I could process what was happening.

As he stood, I reached for the hem of his shirt and he pulled it over his head, tossing it on the floor. He grabbed his wallet, fishing out a condom before shedding his jeans altogether and kicking them aside. He closed the short distance between us, placing the condom on a ladder rung and reaching for me once more. I lifted my shirt, his lips on my breast before I'd even pulled it over my head. I moaned, holding his head close to me as his tongue made tight circles around my nipple.

He lifted his head to kiss me, taking his time by making a long trail from my breast to my collarbone and up my neck. He licked my jaw, eliciting another appreciative moan, before finally settling his mouth on mine. I snaked my fingers through his hair, breathing in the plaster dust I'd loosened, but not giving a damn. The man could kiss. He kissed me in a way that made me almost forget how much I hated him.

I felt behind me and stepped up onto the first rung of the ladder, bringing myself up to his level…and at the perfect fucking height. He grinned as he slid a hand down between my legs. I groaned as I pushed myself into him.

"Fuck, you're wet."

"Shut up. Just don't speak."

He reached behind me for the condom, ripped it open, and slid it on. He raised my wrists, both of us hanging onto the rung above my head, and slid into me, hard as a fucking rock. He grunted as I groaned, and we both began to move at the same time, in perfect rhythm, the ladder shifting slightly beneath me. It was like we were meant to fuck each other. He leaned into my neck, lips brushing against my ear.

"Hailey," he murmured.

I felt his body tense and I loosened my grip on him.

"Don't even think it. Didn't anyone ever tell you ladies first?" I hissed.

"You're no lady."

Still, he released one hand from my hip and slid it between us, finding my clit and rubbing it as he thrust in and out. I lay my head back against the ladder as he fucked me, letting the sensation radiate throughout my body as my orgasm built.

"Pick up your head," he commanded.

I did.

"Look at me."

I looked down instead, watching him move in and out of me as his thumb worked my clit. It was so fucking hot I thought I would come apart at the seams. It was just too much.

"Come for me, Hailey."

I slid my arms past his waist, grabbing his ass and digging my nails into him, screaming his name as I came apart around him. He gave one final thrust and his body seized as he joined me. He pulled out and I stepped down from the ladder, draping my arms around his shoulder as I supported myself against his tall, strong frame. His arms reached around to gather me in, and I instinctively stepped back.

I looked around, found my clothes, and started pulling them on.

"Hailey?"

I said nothing as I dressed, but when I finished I looked up at him.

"Yes?"

He said nothing. I nodded.

"Do me a favour? Start a little later tomorrow?"

I grabbed my coat, slid into my boots, and walked out the front door. Jason and Matt were still outside, but Rob had now joined them. I realized I'd only been in there about fifteen minutes, tops. I cleared my throat as I walked slowly down the stairs. The last thing I needed was—

"Oh my god, you fucked the fireman," Rob said quietly.

"He won't be making any more noise tonight," I said as I walked past.

I turned up my walk and went up the stairs. As soon as I opened my door, I heard the drill start up again. I heard Rob chuckle as I slammed the door behind me.

CHAPTER SIX

Sam

It was after five when I climbed off the ladder and stood back to survey my work. I wiped the sweat from my forehead, admiring my plaster job. The living room was done. I glanced at the ladder, momentarily distracted by the memory of what had transpired there the night before. Hailey was hot, there was no question about it, but she was trouble. And I'd known it from the start. No one to blame but myself.

I walked to the kitchen, opened the fridge, and grabbed a beer. I'd just sunk onto a kitchen chair when the doorbell rang. I hadn't been expecting anyone, and I was a little annoyed at the interruption, but I went to answer it anyway. I didn't even bother looking through the window before opening the door.

There on my porch stood two guys I'd seen in the courtyard. I knew they lived in the house on my right, but I hadn't met them yet.

"Hey, neighbour!" Jason said. "I'm Jason, and this is Rob, my partner. We are the official welcome committee for the courtyard. Normally, we'd have thrown a party, but everyone tends to hibernate in the winter, so we figured we'd just come by and give you the local gossip."

I laughed at that and moved aside to let them in.

"Please, come on in. I was just having a beer. Would you guys like one?"

Rob smiled.

"Yes, please."

The guy was staring at me and making no bones about it. Jason reached out and wrapped his arm around Rob's waist, pulling him closer as he grinned at me over Rob's head.

"Fine, fine," Rob muttered. "I was just looking."

Again, I laughed. I had a feeling I was going to like these two.

"I'm Sam," I said, pulling two more beers from the fridge.

"The fireman," Rob said.

"That's right."

"Well, welcome to the courtyard," Jason

said. "It's a fantastic place to live. Seriously. We've got a great little community going here."

"I could tell by the way Hailey took care of the Levinsons," I observed.

"Yeah. That Hailey is something else. We love her. A little fiery sometimes, but definitely worth getting to know," Jason said. Rob just smirked.

"Well, not sure we hit it off. But I figure as long as we keep it civil, we should be fine."

"Oh? What's the problem?" Rob asked.

"Usual stuff. New occupant, lots of work."

I took a sip of my beer.

"Oh, well, then you should probably get some work done tonight. I know for a fact she's out. I helped her prep for a date, and judging from the way she looked, I'd say she's going to be gone a while."

I choked on my beer and leaned forward as I coughed. Jason whacked me on the back and I caught my breath.

"A date, huh?"

"Yup," Rob said, still sporting that smirk. "You'll find she's out a lot."

I tried to ignore that comment, unsure how I felt about it.

"So tell me about the others. You promised dirt," I said.

Both guys burst out laughing.

"Well, there's Allie and Matt in the house attached to ours. They're fantastic people. We lucked out with them. Between them and the Tates are the Marshalls. Nice couple, too many kids. The Tates, well, you'll hear all about them eventually. Then there's Casey, then Zach. Casey's a kid, house-sitting for the year. Zach is a music producer, hot as fuck, though that probably doesn't interest you... does it?" Rob asked hopefully.

I laughed.

"No, sorry. Next?"

"Right," Rob continued. "Then there's Louisa. She pretty much keeps to herself. Around 40, I guess, divorced and living in her childhood home, which she inherited. Lovely lady, but you'll never see her. And then there's Lily and Chris."

"And who are Lily and Chris?"

Jason smiled and took over.

"They are a very sweet young couple whom Rob here just can't wrap his head around. They were childhood sweethearts and married very young. Lapsed Catholics, but both were raised firmly planted in the church. I like to think they're in recovery mode at the moment and will pleasantly surprise us one of these days."

"You know," Rob added. "Lily has seemed a lot less...high strung lately."

Jason nodded in agreement, and as they fell into a discussion on the topic, my thoughts drifted right back to Hailey and her date. Who the hell was she going out with? I had *just* fucked her. Was that not good enough? What was with this woman? My irritation rose and I didn't notice when the guys stopped talking, waiting for me to say something. I smiled and tried to shrug it off.

"Sorry. What?"

"We were just wondering how the whole fireman thing worked."

*

The guys hung around for a few more hours and several more beers. We ended up ordering a pizza and just getting to know each other. Their easy friendship was rapidly balancing the scales on my Hailey problem. Maybe living here would work out after all.

It was past eleven by the time they finally pulled themselves up off the floor and got ready to head home. It had been a great night. I was glad they'd come, and told them so. That led to hugs. They just wanted to check me out, but I'd had enough beer that it didn't matter either way.

I walked them to the door and we were

laughing about something when Rob elbowed me in the ribs to shut up. He pointed his chin over towards Hailey's and I glanced over. She was sucking face with some dude, clearly enjoying herself. Jason was smiling and shaking his head slowly. He tapped Rob on the shoulder and they went down the steps towards their house. I stood on the porch, watching Hailey go at it with that asshole. After a moment, she broke away and whispered something to him. He stepped back, puzzled. I couldn't see her face—her back was to me—but he did not look happy. He glanced over at me and without a word went down the steps and up the walkway.

Hailey never even turned around, but when she went back inside, she left the door ajar. I went back in and shut my door. I was not going over there. I stood in the vestibule for a minute, struggling. *Oh, who the fuck am I kidding? Of course, I'm going over there.*

I grabbed my keys from the hook and walked out the front door. I trotted up her steps, eased the door open, and walked in. I found her in the kitchen, her back to me.

"That took you long enough," she said, not turning around.

I said nothing.

Finally, she turned and looked me up and

down. She walked over and put her hands on my chest.

"What do you want, Hailey?" I asked.

She purred. She fucking purred.

"You know what I want."

"What's the matter? Your date wasn't good enough for you?"

She shook her head slowly.

"Nope. He didn't make the cut."

"He seemed good enough to suck face with."

She bit her lower lip.

"I know. And that's what left me all hot and bothered."

She ran her hand up my neck to my jaw, then ran her thumb along my lower lip. I took her wrist and pulled it away.

"Sorry," I said. "I'm not into leftovers."

She pulled her hand away and slowly peeled off her shirt. I swallowed, determined not to show a thing. But fuck, she was gorgeous, her magnificent tits gloriously framed by a white lace push-up bra that barely covered her nipples.

"Maybe you're looking at it from the wrong perspective," she said, bending to slide her jeans down her legs and stepping out of them. Her matching panties almost made me lose my mind.

"Oh, yeah? And what's the right

perspective?" I managed to spit out.

"Well, if I were you, I'd be doing everything in my power to erase all traces of him. Fuck me senseless until I forgot his name and screamed yours instead."

She dropped to her knees and got to work on my belt buckle. I stifled a groan.

"I've been drinking," I said, hearing the gruffness in my voice.

She ran her hands over my still-clad erection, which was straining at the zipper of my jeans under her touch. I swallowed another groan. I would not give her the satisfaction.

"Doesn't seem to have affected you in the least," she said, whipping down my pants.

She took me in her mouth and I was fucking lost. As her tongue worked its magic, I couldn't help but fist my hands through her hair, pulling in an attempt to torture her the way she was torturing me. She just purred some more. What did it fucking take with this woman? I could not let her win.

I thrust my hips, fucking her mouth and showing no mercy. But instead of backing away, she wrapped her hands around my waist, bringing me closer and moaning, the vibrations running down my cock.

"*Oh, fuck.*"

I came the second I hit the back of her throat.

She fucking took it like a champ, refusing to let up until I'd completely come down. Then she sat back on her heels and looked up at me.

"Was that so bad?" she asked. "For *leftovers*?"

She stood up and wrapped one arm around my neck, tilting her head up to kiss me. She took my other hand and brought it down between her legs. She was so fucking wet I groaned aloud.

"Show me, Fireman. Do you really come in an emergency?"

I took her mouth. Anything to shut her up.

CHAPTER SEVEN
Hailey

His kiss left me breathless. There was an underlying urgency, like he couldn't wait another second to claim more of me. He dropped to his knees as I had moments before and nuzzled the apex of my thighs. I moaned, grabbing his head. He looked up at me, rose to his feet and lifted me easily. I wrapped my legs around his waist and he walked towards the stairs.

"Stop," I said. "You're not allowed up there."

"I've been in your bedroom, Trouble."

"Not by invitation."

He paused for a moment, then changed directions and walked to the living room. He deposited me on the couch and once again knelt before me. He didn't even bother pulling down my panties, just pushed them aside as he buried his head between my legs. I wrapped my legs around his neck as I rode his face, racing towards my orgasm. It did not disappoint.

He showed me the same courtesy I'd shown him, staying with me until I rode out the last of the aftershocks. He looked up at me and grinned, desire still bright in his eyes.

"You may be a pain in the ass, but you're damn sexy. Especially when you come."

He stood up and pulled me off the couch. My knees were still weak and I stumbled. He grabbed me around the waist, walking me to the dining room and leaning me over the table. I moaned as he peeled off my panties and felt a flood of warmth rushing between my legs. He stood and pressed up against me, hard as a rock.

"Already?" I asked. "You just came."

"What can I say? Fire ain't out yet. I don't quit until the job's done."

With that, he slid into me as he simultaneously brought a hand down between my legs, pressing his palm flat against my clit and applying pressure as he fucked me hard. My breasts were pressed up against the table and all my nerve endings were alive. The pleasure crept through my body, like a low roll of thunder moving through me. I had never felt anything this intense. It freaked me the fuck out.

"Sam—" I whispered.

"You're fine," he said. "I got you. Just hold on and shut the fuck up."

I reached my arms out to either side, grasping the ends of the table. He moved his thumb over my clit as he drove himself into me and my blood turned to fire, coursing through my veins.

"Oh, shit," I screamed.

"That's it, Hailey," he coaxed. "Come for me. Come now."

The orgasm tore through me like nothing I'd ever felt before. Every cell in my body went electric. I swear I saw stars. I could feel him pulsing inside me as he came but I couldn't stop the flow of my pleasure if I'd tried. I was still coming down long after he'd recovered, running his hands up and down my back, caressing my ass.

I turned my head, leaning my cheek against the cool table. I breathed deeply, unable to wrap my head around what just happened.

"I've had sex before. With a lot of different men. That, Fireman, was different."

He pulled out of me and moved away,

peeling off the condom I'd never even noticed him put on. I straightened up and hopped up onto the table, studying him.

"You're awfully good at that, you know?"

He turned to me and grinned.

"So I've been told."

"Yeah, I imagine firemen must get plenty of ass."

He looked surprisingly insulted.

"I'm not a whore, Hailey."

I held up my hands.

"Whoa, easy there. I didn't mean to offend. I've had my share, too."

He grunted and looked around for his pants. I hopped off the table and followed him back into the living room, draping myself over the easy chair and watching him dress. It was a delicious sight. The curve of his ass, the flex of his muscle. I shivered and ran a lazy finger up my thigh. He paused as he watched me.

"You know, most men I've been with aren't in such a rush to get dressed—"

"Stop fucking talking about other men you've been with," he exploded.

I shrunk back, stunned, and eyed him warily. I swung my legs around and planted my feet on the floor, bracing my hands on the chair's arms to help me stand. I suddenly felt very naked in contrast to his state of full dress, but I refused to let that stop me. I got right up, strode past him, and walked up the stairs.

"You know the way out," I said, not bothering to turn back.

*

I woke the next morning to the sound of hammering. I grabbed a pillow and shoved it over my head but it did nothing to block out the noise. Or the vibrations. I threw the pillow across the bed and reached for my phone to check the time, preparing to go next door and tell Sam off. Ten o'clock. Dammit. That was reasonable.

I gave up on sleep and rolled out of bed, heading for the shower. I waited for the water to get hot, then climbed in. As I washed, I thought about the previous night. I'd already broken my first rule by letting him in the house. I never brought men inside. This was my domain. If I slept with them, it was on their turf, where I could easily escape when done. The second rule I'd broken was sleeping with someone in the courtyard. How had I let this happen?

I didn't even like the guy. Sure, he devoted his life to saving people and kittens, but he was a total asshole. Cocky as hell. And really fucking good in the sack. *Shit.* I got out of the shower and dried off, dressing slowly as I considered my options. I should've cut him off altogether, but now that I'd had a taste, I wasn't so willing to give him up. The previous night had been the best sex I'd ever had. I was worried he'd ruined me for other men.

But what the hell was that flare of jealousy? We were fucking. Period. He hated me as much as I hated him, and with that one comment, he cemented my decision to never get tied down. Men thought they could own a woman. Not this woman.

I went downstairs and put on the water for coffee. I needed to clear my head and think. With that in mind, I rolled a joint. Coffee ready, I put on my coat and went out onto the back deck. There was less noise outside and it was easier to relax. I'd have to keep that in mind for the rest of the week. I sat in my chair and leaned my head back against the glass, closing my eyes as the pot seeped into my system. It had been a long time since I'd indulged in a little wake-and-bake, and Allie had given me some really good weed. Vacation was nice.

"Hey, Trouble."

I opened my eyes and shot up, looking over at Sam on the next deck, grinning at me.

"Wanna share?"

I eyed him, hesitating only a moment before getting up and reaching over to pass him the joint. There were just a few inches separating our decks. It was an easy reach. He took the joint but then reached out with his other hand and grabbed my wrist. I looked up at him.

"I thought you didn't smoke," I said.

"I'm on vacation for a week. It's fine." He paused for a moment. "Let me take you out tonight."

I pulled my hand free.

"What? Why?"

"Why not?"

"You don't even like me."

He shrugged.

"True. But maybe it's because I don't know you. I don't even know what you do."

"I own a marketing agency."

He blinked, clearly surprised.

"This shocks you?" I asked, a bitter edge to my voice.

"Yes. But it shouldn't. It makes perfect sense. You're clearly intelligent and driven."

Why was he being nice?

"You don't have to flatter me to fuck me. I'd have thought you'd figured that out by now."

"Hailey. I'm trying to ask you out. Will you go on a date with me?"

I looked him up and down, slowly, taking in every inch. I finally settled on his face, looking him right in the eye.

"No."

I turned around and went inside, leaving him the rest of the joint as a consolation prize.

CHAPTER EIGHT

Sam

A swing and a miss. I smoked the rest of the joint in silence while replaying the scene in my mind. I wasn't even sure what possessed me to ask her out. The woman clearly couldn't bear to be around me unless my face was between her legs. What on earth would we have talked about over dinner?

She owns her own agency.

Why had that shocked me? I'd never thought about what she did for a living before, but it made total sense. The woman was fierce—no reason she wouldn't be successful. But it made me realize how little I knew her. I was keen to spend more time with her, but from where we stood at that moment, it didn't look too likely.

I finished off my day and ordered dinner. I

figured I had a few days left to complete the major work, and I was pretty much on schedule. I pulled the drop cloth off the couch and sat down, flipping on the TV and browsing Netflix.

*

The next morning I was finishing up the plasterwork when the phone rang.

"Sam? It's Principal Bradshaw. I know technically you're off this week, but Jack is asking for you—"

"I'll be right there."

I dropped my phone in my pocket. Another advantage to this house was that it was just down the street from the public school where I volunteered during downtime. I had a few students I shadowed—good kids who just had a rough start and needed a little extra help staying on the right path. If Jack was asking for me, I'd be there for him.

I grabbed my coat and left the house. I walked through the courtyard, waving at Zach on his porch as I went by. Turning onto the sidewalk, I headed north, towards the school. It was a quick, two-block walk.

I found Jack sitting on a bench outside Bradshaw's office. He was a cute kid, just shy of nine with a mop of sandy brown hair, almost like mine. He had a rough home life, which led to some trouble focusing in school. I loved hanging out with this kid. His potential was huge—he just needed a few lucky breaks. I was hoping to be one of them. I took a seat beside him.

"Hey, Jack. What's up?"

He looked up at me, his brown eyes wide with worry.

"Can we maybe go outside?" he asked shyly. I shrugged.

"Sure, it's kind of cold."

"I don't mind."

I stood and he followed suit. He tugged on his jacket and we walked out the front door, taking a seat on the steps. I gave him a minute to collect his thoughts.

"It's a girl," he blurted out.

I had to bite my tongue to keep from laughing. I silently counted to five before replying but didn't look at his face, worried I'd lose my composure.

"What exactly is the problem?"

"Well, everyone in my grade keeps saying she likes me, but when I try to get her attention, she gets real mean. I don't know why, and I don't like it."

His brow was knit together in consternation.

He was seriously bummed about this. The kid was only eight, but I had to take this shit seriously or I'd lose him. I thought for a while before speaking.

"How do you get her attention?" I asked.

Jack looked up at me and shrugged.

"I dunno. I poke her, or maybe tug her hair?"

I gave him a gentle smile.

"Buddy. That's not how you do it."

"It's how my friends do it."

"Your friends are wrong. If you want this girl to like you, you have to be nice to her. Show her you respect her. Don't tease her or hurt her. Maybe instead of poking her, draw her a picture? Or instead of pulling her hair, ask her what her favourite Netflix shows are."

Jack thought about this for a while.

"That's what you do?"

"Yeah, of course. I always—"

Wait. I had long prided myself on treating women well, but that hadn't been the case with Hailey. Fine, maybe I hadn't poked her, but I'd certainly pulled her hair. And instead of getting to know her, I just kept dragging her to bed.

"Actually, kiddo—"

"Hey!" Jack cried. "There's a pretty lady."

I followed his finger to a woman walking

down the sidewalk, approaching the school. A slow smile spread across my face.

"Hey, Trouble," I called.

Hailey looked up and saw us sitting there, surprise registering on her face. She pulled her coat tighter around herself and walked over, eyeing Jack with a curious expression.

"Hey there, Fireman."

"Hailey, I'd like you to meet my little buddy here, Jack."

I elbowed Jack in the side and he looked up at Hailey, stars in his eyes.

"Hi. I'm Jack. What shows do you watch on Netflix?"

Hailey cracked a smile but I burst out laughing. Her expression grew serious and she looked at Jack, then at me.

"He looks like you," she said.

I looked over at Jack and tousled his hair.

"Yeah, he kinda does, doesn't he? Must be why I love him so much." I gave Jack a huge grin, which he returned.

Hailey drew herself up and turned back towards the sidewalk.

"Lovely meeting you, Jack. See you later, Sam. I gotta get home."

And then she was gone. Damn. We had gotten off on the wrong foot. And for some reason, I wanted to fix that. I still didn't know exactly why, but it pissed me off that she wasn't even giving me a chance.

*

I was back home later that evening, waiting on my Indian food to arrive. Another perk of the neighbourhood was the wide variety of small, locally-owned restaurants. We were spoiled, and I was determined to try every joint in the area. When the food came, I brought it into the kitchen and unpacked it, stunned at spread before me. I'd ordered for one, but it was a feast for four, at least.

I considered inviting Hailey over. She'd been pretty cold that morning, but maybe with a peace offering of food, she'd warm up a little. I slipped on my boots and opened the front door, only to be greeted by Allie and Matt.

"Hey," I said.

"Hi, hope it's okay we just dropped by? I'm Allie. I think you met Matt?"

I smiled and shook her hand, and moved aside to let them in. I kicked off my boots and led the way into the kitchen.

"Great to meet you, Allie. Have you two eaten yet? I just had dinner delivered."

Allie walked over to the take-out bag and peered in.

"Oooh! Bombay Mahal! Can't say no to that. Where are the plates?"

I pointed to the paper plates on the counter and she grabbed a few, along with some cutlery. I brought the containers over to the kitchen while Matt searched for drinks in the fridge.

"Beer okay with everyone?" he asked.

I just laughed.

"You guys just make yourself at home."

Allie turned a light shade of pink.

"I'm so sorry, Sam. We're like family here. I know you're new. We've only been here a few months, too. I'm sorry if we're being pushy. Do you want us to go? I just came over to introduce myself."

"No, no, it's fine. Sit, let's eat. It's way too much food. I was actually just going to offer some to Hailey when you came by."

Matt dished out some vegetable korma onto his plate and glanced over at Allie.

"Good thing we came, then," he said. "She's gone."

"Gone? What do you mean, gone?"

Allie shook her head, helping herself to the butter chicken.

"Just for the weekend. She went to some spa with a friend. She'll be back Monday. I think she just needed a little… peace and quiet?"

She looked at me sheepishly. Of course, I was the reason Hailey was driven out.

"No one blames you, dude," Matt said. "You've got work to do. Hailey can be a handful. Don't give it a second thought. Maybe she'll get laid and come back in a better mood."

Matt yelped as Allie kicked him under the table. I let out a little laugh, but inside I was raging. *Laid*? Who the hell did she go away with? But there was no way I could ask without being conspicuous. I forced down the rest of my dinner, no longer tasting a goddamn thing. Monday. That was four days away. And by that time, I'd be back at the station for another week. Which meant I was looking at ten days before I'd see her again.

Crap.

CHAPTER NINE
Hailey

I dropped my towel and slid into the Scandinavian bath, taking a moment to breathe in the cold February air and appreciate the stunning mountain vista of the Quebec Laurentians. I closed my eyes as the warm water enveloped me.

"Liz, this was a phenomenal idea," I moaned.

My oldest and best friend, Liz, was a plastic surgeon and with both of us in high-pressure careers, it was rare we got the chance to escape together. I glanced over at her: tall, curvy, gorgeous locks of red hair. I'd always envied her hair and unconsciously reached up to touch my own.

"I really needed to get away. And with

January behind you, I figured you could use a break, too."

"You have no idea."

"Still having issues with the Fireman?"

Of course, I'd told Liz all about Sam. She was in a long-term relationship with her girlfriend, Tara. Tara ran an erotic website. A while back, she found this writer, Temple Fraser, who wrote these off-the-charts, scorching-hot stories. I was an addict.

I had no idea why Liz and Tara never got married. Neither of them seemed interested. I didn't think either of them had a sentimental bone in their body. Still, I always turned to her for relationship advice. Probably because she was so level-headed.

"I don't know if you'd call them issues. Everything was fine. We couldn't stand the sight of each other and had great hate sex. Then all of a sudden he asked me out. Like, what the hell? We had a perfectly good thing going and he fucked it up."

Liz shrugged and closed her eyes, sliding deeper under the water.

"Maybe he likes you. And clearly, he doesn't know about your…commitment issues."

"I don't have commitment issues. I just don't commit. A few dates, fine. That's it. I have zero desire, time, or energy to get involved in a relationship. I have an empire to run."

"You're going to be lonely one day."

"I'll get a dog."

Liz rolled her eyes.

"Liz, he's an asshole. Even if I did decide to get serious with someone, it wouldn't be him."

"How much of an asshole can he be? He's a fireman! He risks his life for a living," Liz reasoned.

I dunked my head underwater, drowning her out. When I popped back up again, she was staring at me.

"I thought we came here to relax," I said.

"Fine. Whatever."

*

I looked in the mirror, skeptical, but Liz came up behind me and glanced at my reflection. I was wearing a simple black dress, fitted, with a pair of silver and pearl dangling earrings and just a bit of mascara and lipstick.

"You look beautiful," Liz said. "Don't change a thing."

I smiled at her in the mirror and looked at her. She was in a knee-length skirt and a fitted blouse, looking like a knock-out, as usual.

"Why the casino?" I asked.

She shrugged.

"Why not? Great way to blow off some steam."

We left our hotel room and went down to the lobby where we caught a shuttle to the casino. The Mont Tremblant region of the Laurentians was simply spectacular. A little ski village nestled into the mountains, with stunning views everywhere you looked, and tons of people out looking for a good time.

Ten minutes later, we were filing into the casino, the lights and noise surrounding us and making conversation difficult. Liz wandered over to the blackjack table whereas I made a beeline to the poker table. This wasn't our first rodeo and we had already made a plan to meet up at the roulette table in an hour, followed by some serious quality time with the slots.

I surveyed the poker tables, finally settling on one and ordering a drink. I bought in and arranged my chips while the dealer shuffled the cards. A few years ago I'd met this guy, a real heavy metal dude, who played professional poker. In the week I spent with him, he taught me how to play. He'd been great in bed, but the benefits of these skills were far longer lasting and much more profitable.

I played a few hands, winning one, when a guy sat down in the empty seat next to me. He was cute, tall and lean, with dark brown hair and equally dark eyes. He smiled.

"What are you drinking?" he asked.

"Vodka soda."

He signaled to the waitress and ordered two more drinks. He was silent as we played the next hand—he folding after the flop and me holding out until the turn. As the hand played out and the dealer raked in the chips, he turned to me.

"So what brings you here?"

"Um, cards."

He chuckled.

"You alone?"

"Nope," I said. "Here with my girlfriend."

I didn't bother specifying my platonic girlfriend. None of his business. It was strange because had it been a few months ago, I probably would've hooked up with the guy. But I just wasn't in the mood. I'd certainly had plenty of amazing, if rather annoying, sex over the past week and it just didn't seem worth the effort for another empty encounter. Besides, I was enjoying my precious Liz time.

He played a few more hands so as not to look like a total ass, then stood up and changed tables. I never understood people who came to casinos hoping to pick up women. Seemed like an odd choice of venue for such an activity.

By the time I got up from the poker table to meet Liz for some roulette, I was already up five hundred dollars. As I approached and circled the tables, I spotted her gripping onto some guy's arm, cheering loudly. *Nice*. She'd taken in two hundred on the spin. I called her name and she turned to me, pulling me in for a hug.

We played for about another hour before sitting down at adjoining slot machines, each of us nursing a drink. It was late and we were both tired.

"He's got a kid," I said out of the blue.

"What? Really?" Liz turned to me, surprised. "How old is he? How old is the kid?"

"I think he's around thirty-five. Don't know about the kid. Maybe eight or nine? He introduced me to him the other day."

"Huh. And how does that add to the equation?"

I turned and glared at her.

"First of all, there's no equation. Second of all, it just reinforces why there's no equation. I do not need to get involved with anyone, least of all someone with baggage."

"Um, I'm not sure you can refer to a child as baggage."

I just shrugged. Kids were a very vague

concept for me still. A lot of my friends had already popped out a couple, but I just wasn't feeling it. My company was my life. I had built it from the ground up and I wasn't keen to compromise my focus for anything or anyone.

"Whatever. I've got a nice little life going. I don't need any complications."

Liz looked at me and mimed pulling a zipper across her lips. I appreciated the effort.

By the time we left the casino, I was up by eight hundred dollars and I felt like a fucking queen. Liz had broken even, so she wasn't too upset. Especially when I told her we'd hit up a great restaurant for dinner the following night, my treat.

By the time we got back to the hotel, we were both slightly tipsy and giddy with excess cash. I didn't have a thought to spare for any firemen. Nope, not one.

*

We got home on Monday around noon. I dropped Liz off at her apartment and then continued home, looking forward to crawling into bed and having a nap. We'd had massages just before leaving and it had been a struggle to stay awake on the drive. An abundance of Jack White had helped.

I was dreading the idea of construction noise, but I figured if there was, I'd just go over there and demand he stop for a few hours. I'd been gone for four days. He had had plenty of time to get shit done.

I pulled up onto the street and parked, grabbing my stuff and heading inside. As I stepped into the vestibule, I almost landed directly on a piece of folded paper on the floor. I dropped my bags, closed the door, and bent to pick it up. It was a cute little cartoon drawing of a fireman carrying a woman, a few flames thrown up in the background. He was talented and the woman bore a disturbing resemblance to me. On the bottom, he'd scribbled *Back at work. Should be nice and quiet. Rest up for my return.*

I walked to the kitchen and pulled out a Sharpie, prepared to scrawl *I am not a damsel in distress* across the drawing and stuff it back through his mail slot. But at the last moment, I stopped. I kinda wanted to keep the drawing. Then I looked at the note again. What did that mean, *rest up?* Like, for him? What did he think, I was waiting for him to come back and fuck me senseless? If only he knew how many men had propositioned me over the weekend. *Screw him.*

I'd worked myself up into a proper rage

before I realized he probably just meant I should get some rest before the noise started up again. I walked to the living room and paced the floor, wondering which was the more likely interpretation. Then I wondered why the fuck I was wasting time trying to interpret a note, like a fucking insecure teenager. I was Hailey Jacobs, dammit.

I sank into the couch.

What the fuck was going on here?

CHAPTER TEN
Sam

Sunday night couldn't have come soon enough. It had been a hellish week and I was exhausted. After a quick shower at the station, I was anxious to get home. It was after eleven by the time I walked through my front door. I didn't even bother taking off my boots or jacket, walking straight through to the kitchen to make a cup of coffee. Then I stepped out onto the back deck.

It was cold, but not windy. Bearable. It had snowed earlier, and the entire alley looked pristine. By this time tomorrow, enough cars and people would have passed through that it would be black and muddy, but for now, it was pure white. I looked around, the snow and ice clinging to the branches of the trees, the stars shining in the clear night sky.

I smelled the weed before I heard her speak.

"How was your week?" Hailey asked.

I turned to look at her. She was sitting in her usual chair, curled up under an oversized parka with a white hat sitting on her head. One gloved hand held the joint. I sighed.

"It was rough."

She nodded slowly.

I smiled and made the easy jump over our railings. I took the few steps to where she sat and leaned against the railing.

We were silent for a few minutes and I was grateful. Hailey seemed to sense that and wasn't engaged in any of her usual antics.

"So," she said, breaking the silence, "does your kid ever stay with you?"

I looked at her. *What?* What kid?

"What kid?"

"Um, what was his name again? Jack?"

I burst out laughing.

"Jack's not my kid."

She choked on a lungful of smoke. I just kept watching her.

"But he looks just like you," she said, unconvinced.

"It's just the hair, really."

"So who is he?"

I hesitated for a moment. I hated talking

about this because it always led to the inevitable question of why I did it. But for some reason, instead of deflecting her question, I answered it.

"He's a kid I shadow. When I'm not on construction jobs, I spend my downtime volunteering at the school. I work with a few kids each year."

She looked at me, stunned.

"But I was an asshole for being shocked that you owned your own business?" I asked, trying to keep the edge out of my voice.

"Touché," she said.

We were silent for a moment.

"What kind of kids?"

"You really want to know?"

"Yes, or I wouldn't have asked. I'm not in the habit of small talk."

"Right. Well, kids who've had a rough start, or are having a hard time at home. No learning disabilities—I'm not qualified for that yet—but I work at keeping these kids on track, helping them focus in class, being a buddy for them if they need one."

"Not qualified for that...yet?" she asked.

"Yeah. I'm trying to get a certificate. It takes time."

And here it comes...

"Why?"

"I'm cold, Hails."

She huffed and looked around as if debating what to do. She stood.

"Fine. Come in."

She turned and walked through the glass doors. I followed her and slipped off my boots. She peeled off her coat and my heart raced as I took in her figure from behind. She was in leggings and a T-shirt that barely covered her ass. I adjusted my jeans and opted to keep my coat on.

Hailey walked through the house into the living room and settled into the over-sized armchair. I took a seat on the couch. She didn't offer me a drink. I didn't ask.

"So, Fireman. Tell me why you volunteer at a school on your days off, and why you're trying to get certified to work with kids with learning disabilities. This does not match my mental image of you. Explain."

"Explaining is easy. Your mental image is wrong."

She tilted her head, squinting at me. I was finding it difficult to breathe, but I refused to look away.

"I'm willing to concede that might be true. But I need more data."

"Fine. I had a shitty childhood, and I wanted to help kids in similar situations."

She got up from her chair and disappeared into the kitchen. I stared after her, wondering what the hell she was up to. She came back a minute later with a bottle of scotch and two glasses. Without even asking if I wanted a drink, she poured a couple of fingers into both glasses and handed one to me.

Instead of returning to her chair, she sat down next to me on the couch. It was difficult to ignore the heat between us when she was halfway across the room. When she was right next to me, it was fucking impossible. I swallowed, then took a sip of my drink, realizing too late I'd done that backwards. I coughed a little and gave her a quick smile.

"Tell me more, Fireman."

"Jesus Christ, Hailey."

"Just fucking tell me."

I sighed and took another sip of my drink. The truth was, I knew I was going to tell her from the moment she asked. It never even occurred to me to lie or deflect. For some fucking reason I hadn't figured out, I just wanted to be honest with her.

"We were poor. Really poor. It caused a lot of stress at home. My father showed his frustration with his fists. Mainly on my mother, sometimes on me. I'm the oldest of four. Older than my brother by four years. Enough to have been able to protect them all."

I paused, eyeing her and gauging her reaction. She gave nothing away. I emptied my glass and she lifted the bottle to give me a refill, putting the bottle back down on the coffee table and turning her attention to me. She laid her hand on my thigh and looked into my eyes, urging me to continue. I'd completely lost my train of thought, my mind focusing solely on the feel of her hand on my leg.

"When I was in high school, some firefighters came to talk to us about their work. I became obsessed. Started going down to the fire station as a way to get away from home. I'd take my siblings with me, and they'd hang out while I did odd jobs around the station. Those guys took me under their wing and taught me how to be a man, something my father was never able to do."

I put down my glass.

"So, that's why I do it. I figure if I can make a difference for a couple of kids..." I shrugged.

Hailey didn't say anything but drained her glass slowly, never taking her eyes off me. She put down her glass and her eyes swept slowly up my body, from my knees up to my eyes, the air between us charged and heavy.

"That's pretty hot," she said. "Not the childhood part, but the teaching boys to be men. That's pretty fucking sexy."

She pulled her legs up onto the couch and crawled into my lap, straddling me. She cupped my face in her hands, gazing at me with such intensity like she was trying to see who I really was. I opened my mouth to speak, and she leaned in and kissed me.

A million things went through my mind, not the least of which was, *don't do this again*. But it was quickly drowned out by *God, she tastes so good*. I returned the kiss, cupping the back of her head in my palm and wrapping my other arm around her waist. She moved further up my lap, starting a slow grind against me. I could feel myself losing it and I drew back.

"No," I said.

"What do you mean, no?"

"I mean, I don't want this."

She pulled back, surprise registering on her face, followed quickly by annoyance.

"What do you mean, you don't want this? This is what we do."

I put both hands on her waist and easily lifted her off my lap, placing her back on the couch beside me. I stood up.

"Go out with me. Let me take you to dinner. Tomorrow night."

"I don't want to go out with you."

"Why not?"

She sighed, exasperated.

"Because I don't even like you."

"I think you're lying."

She glared at me.

"I'm not fucking lying."

"So why am I here?"

She snorted.

"Because you're really good in bed."

"We've never been in a bed, Hailey."

"Argh. Fine. You drive me crazy with your semantics. You're infuriating, you know that?"

"Go out with me."

"Are you going to fuck me or not?"

"Go out with me."

"NO."

We both stopped and stared at each other, breathing hard.

"I think you should go now, Sam."

I nodded, walked through the house to the back door, and left.

CHAPTER ELEVEN

Hailey

Three seconds after I set foot inside the office on Monday morning, it was like the two weeks of vacation never existed. I loved my work and was proud of the company I'd built, but that didn't change the fact that I was exhausted and worn out. I needed more than a two-week break…especially when one of them was filled with construction noise and confusing hate sex.

I spent the morning going through email and reading all the new client briefs. I allowed myself a late lunch at my desk and was just finishing up when I thought to check the news. I turned to my computer and flipped through a local news site and, with growing dismay, read about the spread of the Coronavirus. Italy was in particularly rough shape. I shuddered to think what would happen if it came here. *When* it came here. The way that thing was spreading…

My attention was diverted by a news story about a fire in NDG. Panicked, I scanned the article for details, relieved to learn it was nowhere near me and that there hadn't been any deaths or serious injuries, though two firefighters had been hurt. My heart stopped for a moment until I remembered Sam wasn't at work. A warm feeling spread through me at the knowledge he was okay, and I clicked onto the next story.

But it was no use. Once that man had penetrated my thoughts, it was too late to go back. Why did I care that he was okay? Obviously, I didn't want him to die, or be hurt, but my body had reacted in a way that was completely beyond my comprehension.

I couldn't believe the fucker wouldn't have sex with me. Who did that? What was with his obsession with taking me out? I had zero interest in dating, and if I did, it wouldn't be with him. The last thing I needed in my life was an arrogant asshole who was gone half the time risking his life. And spent the other half volunteering with primary school children. Yeah. Some asshole.

"Hailey?"

I lifted my head to see Zane, my assistant, standing at the door. Zane was in his late twenties, shorter than the average male, with a mop of light blond hair and piercing blue eyes. He was the most organized guy I knew, and without him, I'd be utterly lost.

"Yeah?"

"Your two o'clock is here."

I shut my laptop and walked to the conference room. I was meeting with a new client I had taken on just before my vacation. It was a new start-up with a dating app that worked like a game show—you answered a bunch of fun questions and it paired you up with someone like-minded. You didn't even see a picture or get an age until you agreed to connect. It was an interesting idea and I had some plans already drawn up for them.

Plus, it was a good diversion.

*

A few nights later, I left the office with a prototype of the dating app installed on my phone. I was in the elevator with Zane when I started looking through it. He looked over, curious.

"The new client?" he asked.

"Yeah," I mumbled, intrigued already.

"How do you plan on testing it?"

"I figured I'd take it home and fool around with it a little, see where it gets me."

"But it's not live. Who will you play with?"

I looked at him and raised an eyebrow. He shook his head vigorously.

"I am not playing the dating game with my boss."

I sighed.

"Fair enough."

I thought about it for a moment, a smile forming on my face before the idea formed in my head.

"It's okay," I said. "I've got just the person."

*

Thirty minutes later, I was home. I walked in the front door and went straight upstairs, throwing on a pair of old, faded jeans and a favourite T-shirt. Being the middle of February, I topped it off with a warm, fuzzy cardigan. I grabbed a hair clip and hooked it onto the hem of the sweater.

I picked up my cell phone from the hallway table and called in an order for Indian food. Then I slipped on my boots and went to ring Sam's bell. He came to the door dressed in paint-splattered sweats and a ripped T-shirt and he never looked hotter. He gave me a wary smile, which was fair considering our current status of…whatever the hell was going on. I ignored the flush of heat between my legs, took a deep breath, and smiled at him.

"I need your help with something."

I couldn't have said *please*? As in, *Could you please help me with something?* I was starting to understand why maybe the guy didn't like me. But it was too late now.

"What's the matter, Trouble? High shelf or stuck jar lid?"

The bastard was smirking.

"Neither. Follow me."

I turned on my heel and went home, not bothering to wait and see if he was indeed following. He was.

I walked through my front door, leaving it open for him. I kicked off my boots and went straight to the living room, where I plopped down on the couch. I pulled my hair up on top of my head, giving it a good twist, and secured it with my hair clip. I watched as Sam came slowly into the room, still eyeing me warily. He took a seat on the chair.

"So? What's up?"

"Can I see your phone?" I asked.

He gave me another odd look but pulled his phone out of his pocket. As he handed it over to me, I put out my hand to stop him.

"Can you unlock it first?"

He grimaced but did as I asked. I smiled inwardly. He handed over his phone and I got to work installing the beta version of the app. When I was done, I handed it back to him.

"Let's play a game. I've got this product to test for work. It's a dating app. You wanted to go out? I'm going to show you there's no point."

A slow grin spread across Sam's face as he sat down. I had him.

"I'm kinda hungry, Trouble."

"Indian is on the way. This is how it works. It's like a game show. People get on the app and are paired up with a game partner. No photos, no bios, nothing. You play this game, answering the questions, and you see how much you have in common. If you both want to meet afterward, you get each other's profiles. What do you say?"

He practically growled.

"I'm in."

I smiled.

"You'll see, Fireman. There's no common ground between us."

We both picked up our phones and started the app. Being the only two, we were paired. First question: *Do you believe in marriage?*

"Shit. Go big or go home, huh?" Sam laughed.

We both hit yes. He looked at me, surprised. I rolled my eyes.

"What? I believe in it. I know plenty of married people who claim to be happy. I just don't want it for myself."

"Why not?"

I sighed.

"Are we going to do this after every answer?" I asked.

"Maybe. The benefit of doing this face-to-face. This was your idea, remember."

"Fine," I huffed. "I'm selfish. I'm self-absorbed. I don't care about anyone else's happiness, and I don't want to feel obligated to. I have a company I built from the ground up and that fulfills me. Sex is easy enough to come by. If I ever get lonely, I'll get a dog."

I looked over at him. He was just staring at me.

"Seriously?"

"Yes. Seriously. Why are you such a fan?"

Sam gazed at me as if he felt sorry for me and I shifted uncomfortably under that look.

"I like the idea that two people can make each other happy. That I can climb into bed every night and wake up every morning next to the same person. That we can support each other and love each other and have fun together."

I shook my head—the idea was completely ridiculous. Who knew he was such a romantic?

"Next question," I said, breaking eye contact.

What's your least favourite position?

Sam cleared his throat and we both typed.

I hit send. *Defense.*

"I think they mean sexual position," he said.

"So do I."

He nodded, understanding.

"Let's move on," he said.

I cleared my throat and looked down at the screen.

Perfect way to spend an evening?

I smiled to myself. *Sitting at home with take-out, either alone or in good company.*

He hit send. *Just like this.*

He looked up at me.

"Not so different after all," he said softly.

We were staring into each other's eyes, both of us wondering where this was going next, when the doorbell rang. I jumped up.

"Food's here."

CHAPTER TWELVE

Sam

As soon she got up to get the door, I went into the kitchen to fetch some plates, cutlery, and drinks. This was not how I'd intended to spend my evening, but I wasn't complaining. By the time I got to the dining room, she'd unpacked all the containers on the table.

"Looks great, Hails," I said. "Thank you."

She looked up at me and smiled. It was so damn hard not to touch her, but I refused to back down on this. The kid had been right. If I wanted her, and there was no denying I did, I had to show her I respected her. I wanted to get to know her. I wanted her to get to know me. I had no idea how I was going to accomplish that until this little experiment of hers fell into our laps.

"Let's keep going," I said.

She looked mildly surprised but grabbed her phone.

"Sure."

Next question. *What's the single most important quality in a partner?*

Easy. *Strength.* I watched as she typed and hit send. *Kindness.* We both stare at each other.

"Let's not even touch that one, It doesn't prove anything," she said.

"Uh-huh."

Next. *Favourite movie?*

I didn't even have to think about it. *Goodfellas.* I waited to hit send until I saw her typing. Her reply came in simultaneously. *Gone With the Wind.* She grimaced after hitting send.

"Let me explain," she started. "I know it's wrong. I know it's a problematic movie. But the thing is, I watched it with my mother every year for decades, and now that she's gone, it's one of those things that makes me feel close to her. So, despite it all, I still call it my favourite."

She looked back down at her screen and then smiled at me.

"But I love *Goodfellas.* It's the only movie I'll always stop to watch when I'm browsing channels. Good call. Next."

That surprised the hell out of me. I had thought she was going to say *Mad Max: Fury Road*. I never expected anything soft and romantic from her. Though there were quite a few similarities between Hailey and Scarlett. I chuckled to myself at the thought.

Biggest pet peeve? Easy. *Stubborn women.* She laughed and typed *Assholes.* I huffed out a breath.

"I thought we'd established I wasn't an asshole."

"Why? Because you fight fires and shadow troubled kids? You can't fool me."

I studied her, trying to figure out if she was teasing me or not. But the more I looked at her, the more I wanted to touch her, so I tore my eyes away and looked back down at the phone.

Dealbreakers.

I stared at her as she typed. When she hit send, I looked down at the screen. *Commitment.*

"Come on. What is it with you? What are you afraid of?"

She just shrugged.

"That's my answer. I told you, I'm not interested."

"I see you, you know. I know there's more to you. Just let me in."

She pushed her food away and stood up, placing her phone on the table.

"Are we going to fuck or what?"

"We're not going to fuck."

She walked around the table until she stood by my side. I pushed out my chair and turned to face her, putting my hands on her hips. She looked down at me, then dropped to her knees. My gut clenched as my dick stood at attention. She ran her hands up my thighs toward my belt.

"You can't tell me you don't want me," she whispered.

I dropped to the ground and leaned in close.

"Of course I want you. I just want more of you."

I stood up and walked away, hands-down the hardest thing I've ever done. I grabbed my coat, slid on my boots, and walked out her front door.

*

I spent the next few days painting and trying to get my mind off Hailey and her stupid dating app. She had intended to prove we had no future but I still called bullshit. There was definitely something between us and I had no idea why she was so reluctant to explore it.

I spent two days that week at school with Jack. He'd listened to my advice and tried a different approach with his girl and apparently, it worked. He beamed with pride when he told me they'd be going to the spring dance together. I suppressed a grin, trying to remember how serious those primary school crushes were.

"How's the pretty lady?" Jack asked as we worked on a math problem.

"Still pretty," I muttered.

"Did you try being nice?"

I smiled again, broadly this time.

"Yes, I did. But I don't think it's going to work as well with me as it did for you, buddy."

Jack frowned, his eyebrows knitting together.

"That's too bad."

"It sure is."

*

Before I knew it, it was March and we were all starting to get a little nervous about the Corona pandemic and how it was going to affect us as firefighters, as well as human beings. After being briefed at the station, I went home feeling heavy, knowing things were only going to get much, much worse before they got better. I'd been keeping my eye on other countries and there was no way we'd escape the same fate. It was just still too hard to believe.

I trudged up my front stairs, dragging my feet every step of the way. I was exhausted. Aside from the usual hectic work week, we were already in the early stages of emergency prep. I just wanted a hot drink, some time on the deck, and to climb into bed.

I walked through the kitchen, filling the kettle and looking for something to put in my cup. I decided on coffee with a shot of whiskey. I continued out through to the back porch, the smell of pot hitting me as soon as I stepped outside.

"Hey, Hails."

"Hey, Fireman. How was the week?"

"Pretty fucking hellish. Wanna pass that over here?"

Hailey stood and walked over to the railing. She looked me up and down, empathy in her eyes. No matter what was going on between us, she knew how hard my job was and never seemed to pull any of her standard shit on Sundays when I came home. It was appreciated. She leaned over and passed me the joint. I passed her my coffee. She dipped her head, sniffed, and smiled. She took a large gulp before offering it back to me.

"That bad, huh?"

"Oh, yeah. This pandemic shit is going to get

serious. I'm just saying."

Hailey said nothing, just reached for the joint, which I handed back to her.

"I'm serious. We've already got cases. Only a matter of time now. They're starting to talk about social distancing. We may be heading the way of Italy. We could be on lockdown before you know it."

She finally turned to me, the smoke curling up past her head.

"You think so?"

"Yeah," I said quietly. "I really do."

"So the world's ending?"

I let out a dry laugh.

"Hmm," she said. She passed me the joint and turned to go inside. "Maybe I should go out with you after all."

She walked inside and slid the door shut behind her.

CHAPTER THIRTEEN
Hailey

It was a dumb thing to say and I had no idea why I'd said it. I kicked off my shoes and took off my jacket, dropping it on the couch on my way through the living room. Instead of sitting, I paced. The truth was, it had been a long time since a man had pursued me like that. Had shown an interest in getting to know me. All of my sexual encounters over the past decade had been casual. I'd never had a man complain he didn't spend enough time with me. They were mostly glad I was gone and hadn't insisted on a cuddle.

I pulled out my phone and texted Sam. I'd programmed my number into his phone when I had it and texted myself at the time. I figured it would come in handy at some point.

Friday night. Seven o'clock.

I waited.

Done.

I went upstairs, got ready for bed, and binged on Netflix until I fell asleep.

*

I spent the entire week in a foul mood. I was short with everyone at the office, even Zane. By Friday morning, he was at his wits' end. He sat down on the chair opposite my desk and gave me a hard look, something he rarely dared to do.

"Okay. Out with it. What's going on?"

"What do you mean?" I asked, feigning innocence.

"You've been in a pissy mood since Monday. Everyone is terrified of you. You haven't met with one client, which tells me you know you're in a shit place and don't trust yourself. So, out with it."

I stared at him.

"Do I pay you to be my therapist?"

"No. You pay me to be your assistant, and I can't assist you unless I know what the fuck is wrong."

I laughed. I loved that kid.

"I have a date tonight."

Zane's jaw almost dropped to the floor.

"Like, with a man?"

"Yes."

"Why?"

I buried my face in my hands.

"I don't know." I looked up at him. "Because he asked? Repeatedly?"

Zane just shook his head.

"Who is the brave soul?"

"My neighbour."

"Jesus Christ, Hailey. Do you really think this is a good idea?"

"No, I don't. That's why I've been in such a shitty mood."

"Right."

I looked around at all the papers on my desk and felt completely overwhelmed. It wasn't like me. I was always in control. I was on top of my shit. Yet as I surveyed the scene in my office, I knew I'd be useless for the rest of the day. All over one fucking date. I stood up.

"You know what? I'm going. I'm taking the rest of the day off. Call the spa and book me an appointment for a massage at one. I'll grab some lunch on the way. Mani/pedi, too."

Zane smiled and gave me a quick salute. I grabbed my coat off the coat rack and walked out the door. I made my way out of the building and down the street, towards my favourite cafe. I had a quick lunch and then spent the rest of the afternoon at the spa. It was the perfect decision. By the time I got home, I was completely relaxed and more than just a little horny.

The bell rang promptly at seven. I wasn't surprised. I'd have been even less surprised to learn he'd been standing out there since five to. But I was ready anyway, so I opened the door to let him in. He looked stunning. Hair slightly tousled, a couple of days' growth. His eyes were clear as he gazed at me. I still hadn't figured out what colour they were. They wavered between the lightest of browns and the darkest of ambers. They were sexy as hell. He cleared his throat and I smiled, stepping aside to let him in.

"Hey," I said. "How it's going?"

"Much better now," he said.

I rolled my eyes. He stopped and looked at me.

"Sorry. Can we start again?"

I sighed.

"Where are you taking me for dinner?"

"Lucille's."

I raised an eyebrow. Smart choice. Close by, great food, good bar. It was a mild night and we both enjoyed the short walk over to the restaurant, which was located right in the heart of the Monkland village. We walked in, got a table, and sat down. He picked up the menu and glanced over at mine, which lay untouched.

"You're not going to eat?"

"Surf and turf. Lobster roll with a half-rack of ribs."

Sam shut his menu and set it aside.

"Sounds perfect."

The waiter came around and we gave our orders, Sam throwing in a bottle of wine. We sat and looked at each other for a few minutes in silence.

"Favourite musical artist?" he asked.

"Jack White."

He nodded.

"Interesting choice. Favourite song?"

"It varies depending on the month."

He laughed.

"Currently?"

I looked him dead in the eye.

"*Love Interruption.*"

He let out an exasperated sigh. I instantly regretted my choice. I wasn't sure why. I tried to make it better.

"What about you? Who's your favourite?"

"Led Zeppelin."

"Fair enough."

Sam laughed loudly and shook his head.

"Well, given your answer, it would've been hypocritical of you to say anything else."

"That's true." I nodded. "Favourite song?"

"*Hey, Hey, What Can I Do?*"

"Nice."

The waiter brought the wine and after Sam gave his approval, he poured us two glasses. Sam raised his, and I did the same. It was a nice wine and the warmth spread through me quickly. I looked him over, taking in the full Sam effect. He was scrumptious. I reached over and lightly traced the back of his hand with my middle finger. He gave me a look and pulled his hand back.

"What about books? What are your favourite books?"

I sighed.

"Why are we doing this, Sam?"

"Because I want to get to know you."

I threw him my most seductive smile and reached out once again, this time tracing a line down his jaw.

"You already know the best parts of me."

He took my hand in his and pressed it to his lips, shaking his head slowly.

"I don't think that's true."

"Well, then, I'm willing to show you *different* parts of me..."

Sam was trying to hold onto his patience. I could tell by his eyes. But instead of stopping, I pushed him further. I was enjoying myself.

"I mean, I've got all kinds of parts you haven't seen yet."

"You are an outrageous flirt."

"Yes. Yes, I am."

"With all the men?"

"Gets me what I want," I smirked.

Sam shook his head once more.

"Won't get me. I want more."

The smirk dropped from my face. I withdrew my hand and straightened in my seat, looking him dead in the eye.

"And what is it you want, Sam?"

"I want a woman who's strong and knows her worth. I want a woman who excites me in every possible way. I want a woman who challenges me, who calls me on my bullshit, and makes me want to be a better man. I want a woman who's independent and capable and won't worry every single time I go out on a call." He leaned in close across the table. "And I want a woman who understands that what we have together will never get old. That the sex will always be explosive and will only get better over time."

He leaned back in his chair and looked me over, taking his time as his gaze dragged over my face, down my chest, and back up again.

"And I think that woman is sitting right in front of me."

I couldn't breathe.

CHAPTER FOURTEEN
Sam

I'd stunned her into silence, which for Hailey was really something. The waiter returned with our food and as he set the plates down, I realized how hungry I was. I picked up the lobster roll and devoured it before Hailey had even finished draping her napkin across her lap. I shot her a guilty smile and took a sip of wine.

"So. Why don't you date? And don't give me the 'I'm selfish' answer because I know that's just a front."

Hailey stabbed a French fry with her fork and nibbled it thoughtfully before replying.

"I don't want to depend on anyone else for my happiness. I don't want to need anyone else to fulfill me. I have my work, my friends, my life. That's what makes me happy. What I do need is sex, and you, my love, will always be welcome to fill that vacancy."

"You know, with my screwed-up work schedule, you'd barely ever see me. Five nights on and I'm asleep while you're at the office. Twenty-four-hour shifts on Sundays. And even on my off days, I'm either volunteering at the school or picking up odd construction jobs. In fact, the number one complaint of previous girlfriends is that I'm never around."

Hailey considered this.

"Interesting."

I watched her eat her ribs. Or rather, I watched her devour her ribs. She was adorable and when she was done, I couldn't help but reach over and wipe a bit of BBQ sauce off her chin. She smiled and reached over to the same for me. I laughed.

"Not the best date food, I guess," I admitted.

"It's perfect."

I smiled and we finished the meal in relative silence, broken only with the odd question and reply. But it was comfortable. For the first time, neither of us was on edge or seething at the other. It was more than comfortable. It was pleasant. And I hoped she saw that, too.

We walked home, the weather still mild, but it was easy to tell a change was in the air.

March in Montreal was tricky and unpredictable. Just when you thought spring was coming, another snowfall would hit. We didn't talk much on the way home. I had a crazy urge to take her hand but even I knew that would be a step too far. I did walk her up to the front door, though.

She looked up at me and tilted her head as if trying to decide what to say.

"This was…not terrible."

I just looked at her, saying nothing.

"I mean, thank you."

I smiled.

She put her hands on my shoulders and tilted her head up slightly, waiting for a goodnight kiss. I still just stood there, silent. She let out an exasperated sigh and collapsed against my chest, her forehead resting against my sternum.

"You're not even going to kiss me," she murmured.

I took her chin in my hand and forced her gaze up to mine.

"Go out with me again tomorrow night."

There was a glint of mischief in her eyes.

"You'll reward me?"

I nodded solemnly, placing my hand on my heart.

"I will."

"Why tomorrow? Two nights in a row is kinda—"

"I'm working a 24-hour shift on Sunday and then I'm on nights. It'll be a week before I see you again. I don't want to wait that long. You'll have too much time to over-think things."

She let out the most incredible laugh; it rolled right off her chest and filled the air, echoing through the courtyard. Throaty and sexy and full of joy. I'd have done anything to hear it again.

"Fine. Tomorrow night."

She turned to open her door and as she walked inside, I followed her. She turned to me, surprised.

"You're coming in?" she asked.

Before I had a chance to think about it, I pushed her up against the vestibule wall and kissed her. She froze, surprised, but recovered quickly and wrapped her arms around my waist. I reluctantly left her lips and kissed a line up her jaw to her ear.

"I'm taking an advance," I growled.

"I'm yours for the taking, babe," she said, pulling off her coat.

I kissed her again, this time with more force. She moaned into my mouth and I pushed up against her. She wrapped one leg around my waist and I grabbed her thigh, grinding into her as she kissed me back. The woman was like a drug for me—I had zero control when we were this close.

I ran my hand up her side, stopping to cup her breast. I drew away, shifting the angle of my mouth before leaning in to kiss her again. She snaked her arms around my neck as I teased her nipple with my thumb. She made a low sound in her throat and dropped her arms, her hands working frantically at my belt.

I let go of both her thigh and her breast, grabbing her wrists in my hands. I had to have some restraint. If I let this go too far, my chances for the next night would be slim. I had to leave her wanting more.

"Hey, hey, hey," she complained.

"I didn't say it was a big advance."

I kissed the top of her forehead and walked out the front door.

*

The next night, I took her for tacos at this little taqueria on Sherbrooke Street. She didn't bother to hide her surprise.

"So, you're done trying to impress me," she said. It wasn't even a question.

I laughed.

"These are great tacos. Tell me you've never

eaten here."

"I've never eaten here."

I rolled my eyes and walked up to the counter and ordered. Then I turned to her.

"How can you judge a place if you've never even tried their food?"

"That's fair."

We sat down at one of the three tables and waited. This place was known for their incredible food, not the speed with which they served it.

"You didn't even ask me what I wanted," she said.

"I ordered one of everything. Not a lot of options here."

That finally got a smile. She relaxed a little and leaned back in her chair, studying me.

"So. A twenty-four-hour shift? That sounds brutal."

"My whole schedule is brutal. You need an advanced degree to figure out how our shifts work. I can pull a Monday-to-Thursday day shift, get a few days off, then a 24-hour Sunday. Or, I can work a ten-to-fourteen-hour night shift. And when I'm off, the only other work I can take is construction really—I don't have a dependable schedule for anything else."

"Sounds exhausting."

"It is. But I love it anyway. I love going to

work. I'm terrified of what's ahead of us with this virus, but I'm happy I'm in a position to help people."

Hailey smiled faintly as she looked at me. I wanted to hear her laugh again, but I'd settle for the softness in her eyes at that moment. I reached out and stroke her cheek. She leaned into my hand and I left it there for a moment, the spell only broken when our food arrived.

We ate in comfortable silence but the whole time I couldn't help but wonder what was holding her back. She clearly enjoyed spending time with me—it was obvious she'd abandoned the idea we hated each other—so why was she so reluctant to give this a shot? Could she have been that stubborn?

After dinner we took a walk, wandering through the alleys of NDG while she told me about her work. She was passionate about what she did, only taking on clients she believed in. It was impressive that at such a young age she'd already reached a place where she could afford to be choosy. She had a staff of fifteen full-time employees and if I had to guess, I'd bet she ran that place like a tight ship.

I resisted the urge to take her hand on the walk, but couldn't stop myself from pressing my palm against the small of her back as we made our way up the courtyard walk towards our houses. When we got there, she hesitated.

"You coming in?" she asked.

I reached over and cupped her chin.

"Depends. Are you inviting me up to your bedroom?"

She let out an exasperated sigh.

"Why is that so important to you?"

"Because I'm tired of having sex on hard surfaces. And I want you to realize the world won't end if you let me in."

I leaned down and kissed her, hoping it would be enough to convince her.

It was.

CHAPTER FIFTEEN
Hailey

Sam followed me through the front door and we both took off our coats and boots, eyeing each other as we did. We walked through the house and I paused outside the kitchen.

"Do you want a drink or something?" I asked.

Sam just shook his head. I took a breath and continued to the stairs. As I started to climb, Sam close behind me, the usual sexual tension I felt around him was replaced by something more like panic. By the time we reached the upstairs hallway, I was having trouble breathing. I stopped outside the bathroom.

"We could fuck in the shower," I said.

He shook his head again, his hand firm and insistent on the small of my back as he guided me towards the bedroom. I swallowed as I walked in, so conscious of him behind me. In my bedroom. My sanctuary. I turned to him and stood perfectly still. My eyes darted around the room desperately.

"Over the dresser?"

Once more he shook his head, walking over to me and slowly unbuttoning my blouse. I sucked in my breath, the panic easing as his fingers worked quickly over my skin. I closed my eyes and felt him lean in, then kiss each of my eyelids softly. I sighed, opening my eyes and putting my hands on his shoulders as he spread my blouse apart, hands all over my breasts. A moan escaped my lips as my hands worked their way under the neckline of his shirt. His shoulders were so incredibly defined; I took my time tracing each line and curve. He reached over his head and pulled off his shirt entirely. I dipped my head and kissed his chest, running the tip of my nose back and forth across his pecs.

He put his hands on my waist and walked me over to the bed. *Sex in my bed.* Again my heart sped up, but I took a deep breath and kissed him, knowing his mouth had a way of making me forget everything else existed. I kept waiting for him to flip me over, to take me, but he kept moving so slowly, peeling off my clothes and laying me on the bed. He unbuckled his jeans and then stepped out of them before joining me. He lay on his side, running his hand slowly down the front of my body, from my collarbone down to my navel. I squirmed slightly, reaching up with my arms to pull him close.

As we kissed, he slid his hand down between my legs and I raised my hips off the bed to meet him. He stilled until I settled down, then slowly started stroking me.

"How do you want me?" I whispered.

"Shhh."

He leaned down and kissed me, and I heard the foil rip as he moved over me. In one motion, he brushed the hair out of my eyes and slid himself into me. I gasped, surprised by both the swiftness and tenderness. He bent his head down, brushing his lips lightly over mine.

"You're so beautiful, Hailey."

I closed my eyes and wrapped my arms around his neck. The look on his face was so tender I could barely stand it. We moved together, slowly, rhythmically, the tension building in both of us. He shifted slightly and I let out a small cry. Keeping the angle, he resumed his movements and I clasped his waist between my legs, my heels digging into his ass.

"Sam…oh, god."

He slowed down a little, easing me away from the edge. I whimpered and looked at him. He just smiled and waited, taking his time before starting up again, bringing me back to the cusp.

"Oh, fuck. Oh, god…" I threw my head back, and he slowed down once again. I wanted to cry.

I tightened my legs around his waist, pulling him closer, thrusting against him, grinding my hips into his. I kissed him, pressing my breasts into his chest, begging him with my body to finish me off. He growled low in his throat and nipped at my neck as he increased his speed, driving himself deeper into me as I screamed my approval. My nails dug into his back as he drove me over the edge, and my heels pressed into him as his hips snapped against mine and I felt his release as he collapsed against me.

We both lay there in silence, catching our breath. Eventually, he rolled off of me and gathered me up against his chest, spoon-like. I racked my brain, but I couldn't recall ever once spooning with a man before. There was something kind of nice about it. It was confusing. The whole night had been confusing. What had we just done? That wasn't fucking. That was way too gentle and tender and full of *feelings*.

Sam brushed the hair away from the back of my neck and kissed me softly. He nibbled on my earlobe and whispered, "Do you want me to go?"

I froze. I didn't want him to go.

"Whatever you want. I don't care."

His arm tightened around my waist and he drew me even closer. I closed my eyes, resting the back of my head against his chest. We both fell asleep.

*

When I woke the next morning, I was careful not to move a muscle. I was instantly flooded with mild regret and gripping fear. I'd never woken up with a man in my bed before. I wasn't sure how to handle it. I took a deep breath and rolled over, prepared to confront the situation head-on. Except Sam wasn't there.

I sat up, sheets falling at my waist, and looked around. He was nowhere to be seen. Had he left? The nerve of him. Fine, it was true, I was planning on kicking him out, but after all that work he went through to get into my bed, he crept out in the middle of the night? And then I heard the toilet flush. I dropped back onto the bed, pulling the sheets up and feigning sleep.

I opened one eye when he walked back into the room, quickly shutting it again when he walked over to the bed. I heard him standing there and imagined him just watching me. It was getting harder to keep still. Finally, he bent over and kissed me on the forehead. I opened my eyes and smiled up at him.

"Taking off?" I asked as nonchalantly as I could muster.

"Yeah. I've got a shift starting soon. I'll be gone most of the week, Hails. I told you—"

I sat up, smiling and nodding.

"It's fine, Sam. I've got a busy week ahead. I wouldn't have had time anyway."

His gaze dropped to my naked chest and I pulled the sheet up, tucking it under my arms. I had no idea why I was suddenly so self-conscious. I was that woman who flaunted her body, not one who hid behind a sheet. But there was something about the way his eyes just pierced right through me, as if he could see what was inside. He cleared his throat.

"Okay, then. I'll give you a call on Friday."

I nodded again, still smiling. He turned to leave, looking back at me as if he wanted to say something, and then walked out the door. I collapsed onto the bed and stared at the ceiling.

What the hell was going on?

*

By Tuesday, it was insane how much I missed him. I hadn't expected him to call or text me, but I was disappointed that he hadn't. And I was really pissed at myself for having that reaction. The whole reason I never got involved with guys was that I never wanted to become dependent, and there I was, waiting to hear from him day in and day out.

At the same time, things were changing quickly in the city concerning the Coronavirus. Every day we were getting new information, along with new warnings on how to proceed. Social distancing was suddenly a thing. The rules on Wednesday were completely different than the rules on Tuesday, and by Thursday everything was complete chaos. When the Premier started talking about shutting down the schools, I gathered everyone in the conference room at work to talk about the next steps.

We had no way to know what was ahead of us, but I figured if the schools were closing and we were heading into lockdown, it was a safe bet to put everyone on work-from-home orders. We spent the day sorting through the clients and campaigns and I ensured everyone knew exactly what their responsibilities were before sending them on their way. I walked through the empty office space, hoping it would be a few weeks at most before we could return.

I packed up my laptop and put a few other things into a box and headed home. It was only Thursday, but I was hoping for some sign of Sam when I got to the courtyard. Nothing. I hadn't heard from him all week, although he'd left flowers on my porch twice. I told myself it was a good thing, that this way I wouldn't get attached or start to see things his way. The more time we spent apart right now, the better.

I ordered Chinese food and settled in for a night of Netflix. For the first time in my life, I wished I had a dog. I was never lonely, but suddenly I found myself wanting to talk to someone about everything that was going on in our crazy world. No, not someone. I wanted to talk to Sam. I picked up my phone and thought about texting him, but he told me Friday. I'd wait.

*

I spent all day Friday setting up a home office in my guest room. I often worked from home

126

at night, so the desk and ergonomic chair were already set up. I just needed a few extra monitors and better lighting. I kept stopping to check my phone, but nothing from Sam. By mid-afternoon, I was starting to get nervous. By dinner, I'd put on my shoes and gone over to knock on his door. I waited and waited until finally, I went over to see Rob. If anyone knew what the hell was going on, it would be him.

I rang the doorbell and Jason answered, talking on the phone and waving a wooden spoon around. He looked me up and down and put the phone on his shoulder, muting the conversation.

"Hey, Hails. Need toilet paper?"

"What?"

"Oh. I figured that's why you were here. Everyone seems to be stocking up and it's not easy to find. You got your supply ready?"

"What the fuck are you talking about, Jason?"

He just shook his head and put the phone back to his ear. Rob appeared behind him and hip-butted him out of the way. He reached out for my hand and pulled me inside.

"What's up?" Rob asked.

"Where's Sam?" I asked, cutting right to the chase.

"He's working this week. Why? What do

you care?" Rob eyed me very suspiciously. I didn't give a damn anymore.

"His shift is over. He should be home by now. The entire city is shutting down. Where the hell is he?"

"Relax. He's a fireman. He'll be fine."

I started pacing.

"Oh, god, he's a fireman. He's always in danger. What the hell was I thinking?"

Rob took me by the shoulders and shook me lightly.

"HAILEY! What's going on?"

I looked at Rob, desperation in my eyes.

"I think I like him."

Rob just looked at me. By this time, Jason had hung up the phone and joined us in the hallway.

"No fucking kidding," Jason said.

Rob just looked at me.

"Hailey," Rob said. "Go home, roll a joint and chill the fuck out. He will be fine. You'll see him when he gets home."

I took Rob's advice. I sat out on my back deck, smoking and looking over at Sam's deck, wondering where the hell he was. I was still checking my phone every ten minutes and I was driving myself crazy. I rolled another joint as soon as I finished the first, hoping by the time I was done, he'd be home. No luck.

I went back inside and threw together some leftovers for dinner. Then I sat down at my laptop and made a huge online order. I was definitely not prepared for a pandemic. I had nowhere near enough booze. I tried to keep myself busy for as long as possible, then I collapsed on the couch and watched horrible romcoms on Netflix until I fell asleep.

I woke to the sound of someone at the door. I opened my eyes and looked around, daylight streaming in through the windows. I figured I must have knocked myself out with the weed. The ringing doorbell persisted and I got up off the couch, touched my hair, decided it was useless, and walked to the door. The closer I got, the more awake I was, and I realized it might be Sam. I ran the last few steps and threw open the door.

It was a fireman, but it wasn't Sam. My heart dropped into my stomach. I tried to swallow, but my throat was dry.

"Hailey?"

"Yes. Where he is?"

The fireman smiled.

"He's okay. Don't worry. Can we sit down?"

I jumped aside and let him in the house. He wiped his feet and followed me into the living room. Like I gave a shit about the floors. I motioned for him to take a seat on the couch and I sat in the chair opposite him. I just stared at him, not saying a word. I couldn't even speak.

"Hailey, relax. It's okay. Just breathe. My name is Mark. I work with Sam. He asked me to come talk to you."

My eyes must have been wide with panic. I still couldn't find my breath.

"Can I hold your hand? You're freaking out."

I nodded quickly. Mark reached out and took my hand. He lightly ran his thumb over the inside of my wrist, which for some reason managed to calm me down a little. When I was under control, I looked him dead in the eye.

"What happened?"

"There was a fire."

I jumped out of my seat, ripping my hand back from his. He stood and took both my hands gently, leading me back down to the couch.

"He's fine. He fights fires all the time, Hailey. He's okay. But a beam fell on him, and he broke his leg. He's at the hospital now getting it set and having a cast put on. He's going to be out of commission for a while. There's a lockdown coming. He wanted to know if you could just make an order for him —he's got nothing in the house—"

"Bring him here," I interrupted.

Mark stopped and looked at me, cocking his head to the side.

"Are you sure? He can take care of himself. He just needs some supplies."

"I said, bring him here."

Mark stood up and nodded.

"Okay. I'll tell the guys."

CHAPTER SIXTEEN

Sam

I sat on a bench in the corridor of the hospital while one of the guys signed me out. I was dirty, broken, and fucking exhausted. All those years with the department and I'd never once been in an accident. My pride was wounded more than anything else. I knocked on my cast, which had finally set, prompting the doctors to release me. All I wanted was to get home and climb into bed for a week. Maybe a shower first. Though I hadn't quite figured out the logistics of that yet. *Fuck.*

Chuck and Greg walked over to me, finished with all the paperwork, and told me it was time to head home. Chuck helped me up, which was more than humiliating, and we walked to the truck. It took me a moment to figure out how to get in, but I did, and I settled in for the ride. The pain meds were still working just fine, so I was all right. We turned up my street and I braced myself for the walk up the courtyard. By the time I lowered myself off the truck, I could barely stand straight or see two feet in front of me. The meds, combined with the physical and mental exhaustion, had just knocked me out. Greg passed down the crutches and I started up the walk.

When I got to the house, Chuck stopped me.

"Hailey wants you to go to her place."

That woke me up.

"What?" I asked, looking towards Hailey's door. "Why?"

Chuck just shrugged.

"Those were Mark's instructions. He's the boss."

I followed Chuck up Hailey's stairs but before we even got to the landing, Hailey was throwing open the door and rushing out.

"Oh my god. Sam. Are you okay?"

She walked up to me and placed her hands on my face. I wasn't quite sure what the fuck was going on, but I wasn't about to argue. I was considering playing up the pain if it was going to get me some sweet sympathy. I rested on the crutches and cupped her face in my hand.

"I'm okay. Don't worry."

She just looked at me with pleading eyes.

"Come inside."

I said goodbye to Chuck and followed Hailey. She'd arranged the living room furniture so the ottoman was in front of the easy chair. She walked me over and stood there as I sat down. Then she knelt and tenderly touched the leg.

"Want me to lift it? I can put it up."

I smiled at her, the drugs making me a little loopy.

"What are you doing, Hails?"

She burst into tears. I sobered right up. I sat up as straight as I could and leaned forward, taking her face in my hands again. I wiped her tears away with my thumb, leaning in to plant soft kisses on her cheek and forehead. She wrapped her arms around my waist and laid her head in my lap. I stroked her hair until she calmed down. After what seemed like an eternity, she looked up at me, sniffling and laughing.

"I'm sorry. I look like an idiot. I feel like an idiot. Sam, I'm so sorry."

"What are you sorry about?"

"Everything. You were right. About us. I was stupid. I spent so much time focused on how I never wanted to take anything from anyone that I never realized how much I had to give. This whole week was horrible without you, and then when I found out you were hurt? It's like my whole world came crashing down. Nothing mattered. All I wanted was to know you were okay and to have the chance to take care of you."

She stopped to take a breath and I couldn't help but smile. I wanted to interrupt and put her out of her misery, but I also really wanted to hear what she had to say. I had a feeling this was not standard Hailey operating procedure.

"Sam, if you're willing to give me a chance, to give this a chance…to forget all the horrible things I said to you and see if we can make something with this…I'm in. I'm all in."

She sat there, back on her heels, staring up at me with eyes so sad and round. I studied her for a moment, watching her neck move as she swallowed, the way she brushed the hair from her face. She looked so unsure, so vulnerable. She was just so goddamn beautiful. I reached for my crutches and pulled myself into a standing position. She got up, standing right in front of me, still gazing at me with those soft eyes.

"I don't know, Hailey. You were pretty rough—"

Her eyes widened and filled with panic. It

was all I could do to suppress my smile.

"Sam, I swear—"

I grabbed her by the hips and pulled her close.

"I'm kidding. Of course, I want to give this a chance. I'm crazy about you, Hailey."

She smiled and kissed me. I moved my hands to her face and deepened the kiss. She sighed, never breaking contact, and wound her arms around my neck. I don't know how long we stayed like that, but by the time she pulled away, we were both breathless. She motioned to the cast.

"What does this mean?" she asked.

I looked down at it.

"It means I'm off for at least six weeks."

A slow smile spread across her face.

"You know we're going into lockdown, right?"

I smiled.

"I do."

"If you quarantine with me, I'll take care of you."

I ran my finger down her jaw, stopping at her chin and tilting her face up to look at me.

"Will you now?"

She gave me a wicked grin.

"First item on the agenda is figuring out how to, you know, with that thing on."

I laughed.

"First item on the agenda is figuring out how to shower with this thing on."

She got up on her tiptoes and whispered in my ear.

"I like you dirty."

I groaned and closed my eyes for a second. Then I took her hand and grabbed my crutches.

"Take me upstairs, woman. We've got work to do."

Other books by Sydney Campbell:

Allie Styles Romance Series:
Temptation (Book 1)
Deception (Book 2)
Reckonings (Book 3)
Beginnings (Book 4)

Courtyard Tales of Contemporary Romance
Reawakening
Redemption
Reckless